New Sex Story (2 Books in 1)

My Christmas Wish(Lesbian) + PLEASE LOVE ME

Catherine harbors romantic thoughts for Vanessa

Explicit Erotic Sex Stories

My Christmas Wish(Lesbian)

A tale of friendship, love and the magic of a Christmas wish.

Pamela Vance

This is a work of fiction. Names, character, places and incidents are either the product of the author's imagination or are used fictitiously, and any resemblance to actual persons, living or dead, business establishments, events or locales is entirely coincidental.

@ COPYRIGHT

All right reserved. No part of this book may be reproduced or used in any manner without written permission of the copyright owner except for the use of quotation in a book review.

I actually knew Aubrey from college.

Well...I didn't exactly 'know-know' her, but rather knew of her. She was two years ahead of me in school and was a big presence on the college party scene. Not that she was like the campus drunk or a slut or anything - at least not that I was aware of, but basically if you happen to be one of the hottest girls on campus - which meant you were one of the hottest girls in the whole college town - then people tended to pay attention to pretty much everything you did. Those same people also liked to comment on Aubrey...and gossip about her...and cater their own plans around what she did. I thought it was silly and kind of weird that some of the people I hung out with were so interested in whether Aubrey was going to a particular bar...or if she was at a certain function...or if they had heard from a friend of a friend that she may or may not be going to a party or not...yeah, you get the drift.

Anyways, I never got caught up in the whole Aubrey-watch thing. I basically just partied wherever I felt like going and with whoever happened to be there and had fun...but not too much fun. I also didn't date much because I honestly didn't see the point in complicating my life with a boyfriend. I'd never even had a serious relationship. I suppose I wasn't all that interested in one because I'd just never met the right guy. I got asked out often enough, but no one triggered the desire in me to get all serious and committed. I mean, I dated and went out and had fun...but like I said, nothing serious.

Besides, my focus was on my education and school wasn't cheap. I was mature enough to understand that every class, lecture and book was a cost to my parents. They worked hard to send their only child to this expensive private college. I figured that if they were going to go out of their way for me to attend college and not have the burden of student loans when I earned my degree, the very least I could do was work hard at being a good student. This might be one of the reasons why I graduated Magna Cum Laude. My parents were very proud of me for that...and I was too.

Apparently prospective employers weren't nearly as impressed with my accomplishment as I hoped they would be. I mean it was mentioned as "impressive" in more than a couple of interviews, but I quickly discovered that actual "real-world work experience" was much more preferable. So for the summer months after graduation I kept busy with a couple of part-time jobs while I continued my job search. I loved my job at the animal rescue, but absolutely abhorred working retail. I'd much rather spend my time caring for dogs rather than seeing the worst of people as they shopped for clothes...but it paid the rent.

Fall and winter are my favorite seasons of the year, so as summer came to a close I refused to let myself get discouraged despite my failure of finding full-time employment in the career field I'd just spent the past four years of my life learning how to do. I knew it was only a matter of time before someone gave me a chance, and when they did I was going to run with it. I kept working and filling out applications and going to interviews and during the middle of October I had what I thought was an 'okay' interview. I was actually surprised when the recruiter called me a week later for a follow-up interview. I tried to temper my excitement and not get my hopes up, but I have to say I ended up nailing that second interview. The company offered me the job right there on the spot...I was over-the-moon thrilled that I finally landed a job in my field.

My new job also happened to be how Aubrey and I crossed paths again.

Like I said, we really didn't 'know-know' each other so after I was hired to work in the marketing department for this large distribution company, you can imagine my surprise. It was my first day of work after working my two weeks' notice at my other jobs. I had just finished filling out all of my new-hire paperwork in the office of the HR manager when my new boss popped in. He wanted to welcome me and take me on an official tour. My first impression of the Director of Marketing was that he came across as a nice guy. I made sure to pay attention as he introduced me to my new co-workers. Everyone at the company he introduced me to seemed to genuinely like him...I took that as a good sign that my instincts about my new boss were right.

My tour meant we ended up walking around the entire company campus which consisted of two office buildings, a warehouse and a fabrication shop. I met and shook hands with every single employee who worked at the corporate location, but my boss saved the formal introduction to the actual Marketing Team for last. I followed him into the designated section of the second floor of the main office building into what was considered the Marketing Department proper. Yep, there was Aubrey, sitting at her work station. I had no clue that she'd been a marketing major same as me.

I was introduced to everyone on the team as the new marketing specialist and Aubrey greeted me warmly with a smile that included a hint of recognition when we were introduced. I was also shown around our little part of the company world. It was good to know where the restrooms were, where the coffee service was and the supply room that was exclusive to marketing. It also didn't take a rocket scientist to realize that the only empty chair was right next to Aubrey's. So after getting a lay of the land, shaking everyone's hand, repeating my name about a dozen times and trying to remember everyone else's, I was formally shown to my work station.

Aubrey was working on some kind of excel spreadsheet as I sat down next to her, but she stopped and turned to me with a hint of a smile and one of those knowing squints of recognition. "Wildcat?"

"I am," I smiled.

"I thought I recognized you," she nodded and her smile grew.

"Yeah, I thought I recognized you too," I nodded. "Small world, I guess."

"Definitely," she laughed. "When did you graduate?"

"This past June...class of 2015," and I blushed but wasn't sure why. "Is it that obvious?"

"Not at all," she shook her head and then smiled again.

Two things were running through my mind at that moment. The first was that there should be someone standing around handing out sunglasses to prepare people for this girl's dazzling smile. That and I think I had an inkling of understanding of why people liked to hang around her back in college. She had this effortless way of putting you at ease without really trying.

"Welcome aboard," she sat up straight and extended her hand. "I'm Aubrey."

"Thanks," I nodded and shook her hand. "Meghan."

"You're going to love it here, Meghan," she raised her eyebrows knowingly. "This is an awesome place to work."

"Yeah, it seems great so far," I agreed with her even though I didn't have the first clue about what it was like to be an employee here. I had been on the job for like two hours, but I guess I was just going to take her word for it.

Aubrey turned back to her spreadsheet with one final smile so I went through the process of booting up my laptop. Everyone in the Marketing Department had a company supplied laptop with a docking station at their desk. Made it so easy - you had the flexibility and mobility of a laptop, but you could dock it and use the mouse, keyboard and large flat screen at your work station whenever you were in the office.

I settled in and remembered that I had been politely instructed by HR that I absolutely had to complete my mandatory new hire training on the company intranet by no later than my third day of employment. I was eager to start working, so I went ahead and followed the instructions on the home page and fired up the first video. When I was finished 25 minutes later a five question quiz popped up on my screen. I aced it. So that was how this was is going to work...you had to watch videos and then take a brief test that showed that you actually watched the video and paid attention. I looked at the que of my assigned training, did the math in my head and realized I'd be watching videos for the rest of the day and most of tomorrow. The videos ranged in subject matter from how to request paid time off, to how to evacuate the building in case of an emergency as well as Slips, Trips and Falls safety and what the proper dress code was in various types of weather. There was a training video for pretty much every conceivable work-related topic I could think of.

I sighed quietly to myself as I started up the next video lesson.

My first day was a haze of videos and quizzes. I don't even remember going out for lunch or what I ate. Finally, the clock seemed to be winding ever closer to the end of the work day, but I was still steady at it. I wanted to get these training videos out of the way so I could get my feet wet with some real marketing work. I had just finished up another module and while stretching my neck glanced at Aubrey. I realized that with the curve of the counter as it turned the corner that acted as the table / desk of our work stations that my seat was at a slight angle and behind hers. If we were both sitting straight on facing our computers, I could turn my head to the right and basically see over Aubrey's shoulder to whatever she was working on...and she was currently busy texting on her cell phone. I ignored her and turned my attention back to my own pc and started the next training video. Out of the corner of my eye I saw her look slyly over her shoulder at me to see if I was watching her. She smiled.

Huh...she seemed to be acting like, I don't know...like she was up to something? Whatever...I clicked the button to start my next video.

****

Before I knew it, my first week was in the books and Aubrey had been right - I really liked it here. The people were great, the company was awesome and as a sales driven organization, they kept the marketing department very busy. My first assignment was a simple sales report for the previous quarter and I knocked it out of the park in a few hours. I guess that was going to be my one and only "introductory" assignment because after that my workload was just like everybody else's in my department - crazy busy. But I loved it - I thrived in that whole multi-tasking, deadline looming environment and that's pretty much what I did every day.

I also ended up learning a little more about the meaning behind Aubrey's sly little smile that first day.

I was busy working on a campaign proposal towards the end of my second week. I was frustrated as I tried to think of some alternative sales slogans for this campaign. We were going to start offering a new product from one of our vendors and I was trying to get my brain to think outside of the box, so I just kind of let my eyes wander around my work station. I ended up looking at Aubrey or rather over her shoulder as she was playing with her phone. She was leaned back in her chair and I could see her screen. She was texting and from what I could see it looked like she was sending someone a picture.

Absentmindedly I went ahead and let my eyes focus on the screen of her phone. Huh...a selfie? Surprise, surprise...yep, definitely a picture of Aubrey...wearing the same outfit she had on today...only in the picture she was in the ladies room (I recognized the color of the walls)...and she had her shirt unbuttoned flashing her bra covered boobs to the camera. I couldn't help but lean forward a little and stare. Uh...wow...but in my head it was more like WOW.

It was about the only word I could think of.

I'm not a lesbian or bi or anything, but there was no denying the girl is drop-dead gorgeous - like movie star level gorgeous. First off, she has this long, thick mane of amazing chestnut-brown hair and these deep, amber-brown eyes. Plump, pouty lips and the kind of flawless face you see on TV...like I said, gorgeous. Secondly, I don't know if she owns her own tanning bed or what, but she has this really great tan complexion. Okay. Good for her, right? Oh, but the topper is this chick's body...I mean, give me a break already - it's one thing to have an unbelievable ass - which Aubrey does. I'm talking a world-class ass...but did she also have to be blessed with big boobs? Like perfectly shaped, just freaking awesome big boobs from what I could see of that picture.

I mean, c'mon, man - in what universe is that even remotely fair?

I was so busy creeping over her shoulder at that picture that I was completely unaware that she had turned her head and busted me. When I finally realized she was looking at me, I sat back and could feel my face get really hot from what I knew was the blush creeping up my cheeks. Oops. I felt like such an asshole. I mumbled an apology and turned back towards my computer when I felt something nudge my shoulder. It was

Aubrey's hand holding her phone. She nudged me again like she wanted me to take her phone.

"Is this too much?" she asked with raised eyebrows and that same sly smile I had seen my first day on the job. "Honest opinion."

"Uh...okay," I slowly took the phone and glanced down at the picture again. My goodness, but this chick was freakin' built. I cleared my throat and then looked up into those mischievous brown eyes. Was she just trying to show off or did she really want my opinion? "I guess it kind of depends on what you're going for."

"I was going for tease," Aubrey whispered with an uncertain look on her face. She took the phone back and cast a quick glance over her shoulder towards the Marketing Director's office to make sure his door was still closed. She bit her lip and with another quick glance at me, started manipulating buttons on her phone. After a minute she seemed to find what she was looking for and passed the phone to me again.

I took it from her and looked at the screen and saw that she had opened up a gallery of pics. There were five different pics and based on the outfit and background, they were all taken today in the ladies room. I scrolled through them and saw that it was basically a photographic progression of her shirt being unbuttoned, exposing her bra a little more in each image and then in the final pic (the one I had seen over her shoulder) she was pulling her shirt open to reveal both of her bra-clad breasts. I probably stared at that picture for a little longer than I should have, but I was so envious. I mean, damn!

"So?" She finally interrupted my pervy examination of her pictures. The uncertainty in her tone of voice and the apprehensive look on her face seemed out of place from the perception of Aubrey I had in my head from college. "Which, uh, which one?"

"Well," I replied slowly and had to clear my throat. "If you're going for tease, then...I think the third one."

"Really?" Aubrey seemed surprised. She took the phone back and looked at the image I had indicated with a slight scowl. The picture was the one where she had almost all of her buttons undone and the viewer could see obvious cleavage and the front part of her bra...but only a hint of the actual bra cups and the mind-boggling boobs they held in them. "I thought that one was...I don't know, kind of tame."

"Well...think about it from the viewer's perspective," I explained and noticed she was listening intently. "You're giving whoever this person is looking at it just enough of a suggestive glimpse. You said you wanted to tease them, so don't give away too much. Leave'em wanting more...it'll drive them crazy."

"Crazy, huh?" Aubrey considered what I said for a moment and then the thoughtful expression on her face slowly changed into a grin. "Okay...yeah, I like that. Thanks, Meghan."

"Anytime," I shrugged and turned back towards my computer.

A few hours later Aubrey invited me to go to lunch with her and since I didn't have any plans, I agreed.

I think we were both surprised at just how much fun that meal was and how well we got along. It turned out we actually had a lot in common. We went out to lunch again the next day and it was the same. So we started going out for lunch all the time and we even began sitting together in the break room whenever we happened to pack our lunches. It didn't take long before we were pretty much inseparable at work...and as cliché as it sounds it was once again proven to me that you just can't judge a book by its cover.

The more I got to know Aubrey the more I realized that under all that incredible beauty and sexual hotness was a genuinely nice person. I mean, she was really great and I really liked her. She went out of her way to make sure I knew everything I needed to know in our department to be successful...who you could bullshit and who you couldn't, how and when you could slack off for a short break. I never expected it, but Aubrey ended up being one of the sweetest and most thoughtful people I had ever known.

Now I'm not considered unattractive by any stretch of the imagination. Blonde, blue-eyed, I'm very petite with a nice figure if I do say so myself. I've basically been called cute and pretty my entire life ever since I hit puberty...but it was really amusing to be a first-hand witness to all of the attention Aubrey got whenever we were out. I became pretty much invisible. It was crazy how both men and women would just fall all over themselves to help her or take her order or get her whatever she needed. I guess maybe since she looked just as attractive as the celebrities on TV and the internet that most people just kind of assumed she was one. Most of the time Aubrey acted like she didn't notice it, but she wasn't above taking advantage of the preferential treatment every now and then...especially if it meant a better table at a restaurant or someone buying her drinks. She didn't act like it was a big deal, so who was I to complain about it?

Hanging out at work was a no-brainer since we literally sat next to each other, but then we started going out after work and it didn't take too long before we started hanging out on the weekends, too. I found myself really enjoying spending time with Aubrey. She made even the simplest things like just sitting around and watching TV fun...but when we did decide to go out? Man, she was an absolute blast to party with. I don't know if she was just used to getting away with stuff or what, but I learned pretty quickly that when this chick got a little too much alcohol in her she became something of a wild child...and a troublemaker. More than once I ended up being the voice of reason and would get her home safely before she ended up doing something she regretted.

In just a short amount of time we became not just work friends, but really good friends.

****

Shortly after we had started hanging out away from the office, Aubrey got invited to what was supposed to be this really cool party by some guy she had met at some bar. There was kind of a social lull among the crowd we usually hung out with now that Halloween had come and gone, but Thanksgiving was still a week away. Aubrey thought it would be fun and since neither of us really had anything else to do she insisted that I go with her. It turned out that this party was downtown in the penthouse suite of one of the high-rise buildings in what I knew to be extremely pricey condos, really fancy-schmancy. We got all dressed up and it did end up being pretty cool...we met some nice people, the food was crazy good and they had a full-service bar and a DJ. What was not to like?

We were definitely intent on enjoying our evening as both Aubrey and I were drinking, her maybe just a skosh too much. I slowed down my intake and made it a point to keep my eye on her. After a while I'm standing there just kind of watching her as she stood with her back to the bar amidst a small crowd of people. She was of course the center of attention. I occasionally nodded my head to the guy next to me as he droned on and on about his boat. Really? Dude, its November....but I was trying to be polite so I stood there and half-listened. My eyes moved down the bar away from Aubrey and for some reason I settled my gaze on the host of this party. I watched as he concentrated on putting together a tray of shots. I guess what got my attention was the fact he was using real glass shot glasses and not plastic cups.

I continued watching with a little more interest when I saw him look around over both shoulders, but in a sneaky kind of way...like that wasn't suspicious. I scowled as I watched this douchebag empty the contents from what looked like a small vial or some kind of pill bottle into one of the shots. I found myself stepping away from my would-be suitor in mid-sentence. I began to walk across the room, stepping around party guests and mumbling 'excuse me' while keeping my eyes glued to the asshole host as he carried that tray of shots over to a group of people. The same group of people who were hanging around Aubrey. I was having a hard time believing that this was actually happening as I approached the group.

Unreal. He actually did it...I literally watched him do it. He made sure Aubrey got the doctored shot. I didn't have time to explain or intervene, so I did the only thing I could think of - I lunged into the middle of these people and slapped the shot glass out of Aubrey's hand. I actually slapped her hand a little harder than I meant to as she yelped and immediately clutched her hand to her chest in pain. She looked up at me in shock and I started to reach towards her to explain when the wannabe rapist prick blew his top.

"Hey!" the douchebag-host stepped in front of me and looked at me like I had lost my mind. "What the fuck?"

"She's my friend," I replied a little too loudly. As far as explanations went that really didn't make a lot of sense, but my adrenaline was pumping. I leaned to the side of him so I could look at Aubrey. "Come on, time to go."

"Oh, hell no!" the asshole glared down at me and raised his voice. "Bitch, I'm telling you right now that you aren't going any-fucking-where until you clean this up."

"Yeah, about that," I raised my voice and turned my full attention to this motherfucker who just happened to be about a foot taller than me and twice as big. I didn't care. I was furious and a little drunk. "I could care less about your fucking carpet since you were trying to drug my friend with that shot...bitch!"

The crowd around us within earshot of my voice immediately got a lot quieter and turned all of their attention to the scene unfolding in front of them.

"What?" the host replied and he suddenly seemed more nervous than pissed. "I don't know what the hell you're talking about...but you're gonna pay to have my carpet cleaned."

"You really think so?" I asked doubtfully. I reached down and picked up the shot glass that still had some remnants in it. "Huh. I wonder if the cops can test this...you know, see what all is in it."

He started to laugh, but then his hand shot out and grabbed my wrist hard enough that it made me drop the shot glass. With a jerk on my arm he pulled me in closer and lowered his voice. "Whose fucking house do you think this is?"

"Let...go." I demanded quietly and tried to pull away. He just smirked at me as he held on. I looked him square in the eye and told him straight out, "You're hurting my arm. I'm asking you for the last time...let go of me."

With an even bigger smirk the asshole nodded his head and did as I asked. He let go by giving my arm a push which sent my little ass tumbling backwards to the floor. Everyone just stood there in shock and a few people let out a quiet "hey" in protest. I started to get up and was all prepared to try and kick him in the balls when a large brown hand shot in from stage left of this little drama and grabbed the douchebag by the throat. The guy froze and his eyes got really big. He reached up to grab on to the hand that was around his throat, but it didn't look like he was doing much but hanging on. I glanced down and saw that he was being lifted up onto his tippy-toes.

My eyes followed that large brown hand to the brown face it belonged to and hey, it was that nice, unbelievably humungous guy that I had chatted with earlier. I thought he was really nice. During our conversation I remember he mentioned that he was

Samoan...and, oh yeah, I think he also mentioned that he played for one of the NFL teams.

"You hurt?" he asked me simply. My arm would probably end up being bruised, but nothing serious. I shook my head no.

"You?" he next asked Aubrey. She was wide-eyed and slowly shook her head.

"You ready to apologize?" he asked the piece of crap in his grip.

Douchebag managed to sort of nod his head and then croaked a strangled, "Sorry."

Humungous Samoan dude let go of the guy's throat and the douchebag immediately went to his knees. He brought both of his hands up to hover protectively near his damaged throat as he started coughing and gagging. The whole party erupted into applause and people started high fiving the pro football player. I turned to Aubrey. She nodded. It was definitely time to go. We made a beeline for the door and I called a cab from the elevator. We were both a little shook up, but we still managed to laugh at the fact that chivalry was not dead.

We got in the cab and I gave the driver Aubrey's address to drop her off first. She told me to just stay at her place tonight. We could do a late breakfast in the morning. I hesitated, but then she asked me to please stay, that she didn't feel like being alone after all that bullshit at the party. I finally agreed and we both just kind of rested in a comfortable silence in the back of the taxi as it headed towards her apartment. I ended up having to help Aubrey up the steps...she was a little drunker than I thought.

It was also later than I thought.

I was exhausted and asked Aubrey if I could borrow a t-shirt to sleep in. She nodded towards a drawer as she headed for the shower. She announced that she wasn't going to wash her hair as she put her long tresses up into a ponytail-bun, but she wanted to wash the stink of that party off of her. I stripped down to just my bra and panties and threw the oversized t-shirt on. I was crawling under the sheets of Aubrey's queen size bed when I heard the shower shut off.

I settled down under the fluffy comforter and was in the process of reaching up to flip the pillow over so that I could lay my head against the cool side of it when Aubrey walked into her bedroom with a just a towel wrapped around her. I could see from the glow of the little night-lite by the door that the tan skin of her shoulders glittered from little droplets of shining water on them as she walked around to the side of the bed I was lying on. She sat down next to me on the edge of the bed and silently looked down at me for a moment. She smiled and I could tell she was still buzzed. Suddenly there were tears in her eyes.

"Meg..." Aubrey whispered as she tried not to cry. "I just wanted to say thanks."

"Hey," I sat up and wiped away a tear from her cheek with my thumb. "No worries, hon."

"I'm serious," Aubrey insisted as another tear ran down her cheek.

"So am I," I smiled and wiped that tear away and then took her in my arms in a reassuring hug. "I got your back, Aubs. That's what friends do...they lookout for each other."

"Thank you," Aubrey whispered and then stood up. She gave me another tired smile as she walked back around to her side of the bed. She took the towel off and wiped her face with it and then crawled into the bed next to me...without a stitch of clothing on.

I was stunned. I mean, it wasn't like I had never shared a bed with another girl before. It certainly wasn't the first time I had seen one of my friends naked either. Hell, it wasn't even the first time I had slept in the same bed with a naked girl...it was just Aubrey without clothes on was - fuck, I don't even know how to describe it. A work of art? Beautiful beyond description? I mean she was utterly stunning.

"I really appreciate you being my friend, Meg," Aubrey whispered as she faced me. "I really do."

I turned towards her and whispered back, "I really appreciate you too, friend."

She grinned and then let out a big yawn. "I'm really tired."

"I know, baby," I whispered. Baby? Why did I call her baby? "Just try to get some sleep."

"Mmmhmmm," she mumbled in agreement and turned over on to her other side facing away from me.

I was still kind of in shock from seeing my goddess-like friend completely naked. Wow...Aubrey was ridiculously good-looking and extremely attractive with clothes on, but naked? Holy smokes - that's like a whole other level of hotness. I closed my eyes and mentally shook my head at the events of the evening when I felt Aubrey scooch back into me. I gently started to move backwards away from her when she wiggled her ass until it was pressed right up against my groin area. She reached behind her and grabbed one of my arms and then pulled it around her so that I was spooning her tightly.

I tensed up for a moment, but then relaxed and with a small sigh snuggled her close to me. My friend needed to know that I had her back and I was there for her. She obviously needed to be comforted right now...she needed to feel safe and loved. I was also still kind of buzzed...that was what I was telling myself.

Yep...I was totally chalking up that little tingling feeling in my panties to the alcohol.

****

I was warm...and comfortable...and slightly hungover.

I managed to open one of my eyes and found myself staring directly into the tangle of Aubrey's hair. I did a quick inventory without moving. Stomach just the littlest bit queasy, but I think after I had something to eat I would feel better. My head hurt and my arm was a little sore, but not unbearably so. Ibuprofen or aspirin would help that. Uh, wow, I became aware that part of that warmth and comfort was due to all of the intimate body to body contact. My leg was kind of thrown over Aubrey's leg and she had her naked butt nestled right up against my lady parts.

My arm was draped over and kind of around her waist and...yup, that was definitely a handful of Aubrey's large breast resting in my palm. Her breast was heavier than I would have thought...and really firm, but still really soft. It actually felt quite nice.

I can honestly say that I'm not really sure exactly why I did what I did...I think it was probably due to the fact that I had never felt another woman's breast before. I mean not like felt 'for real' in such an intimate setting as the one I was in now, all cuddled up with my naked friend in her bed. So yeah...I did it. I gave Aubrey's breast a nice squeeze as I closed my eye and dozed back off.

I have no idea how much later it was when I woke up again, but I didn't feel quite as rough and the space next to me in Aubrey's bed was empty. I gradually managed to sit up and swing my legs around so that my feet were on the floor. I was still hungover, but not as bad as I expected to be. I definitely needed food and something for my headache and my sore arm. I stood up and took two steps towards the bathroom when the door opened and Aubrey stepped out dressed in yoga pants and a t-shirt drying her hair with a towel. It amazed me that she could look that good with no make-up on and wet hair.

She immediately smiled at me and quietly said, "Good morning."

"Morning," I smiled back and went to move past her so that I could relieve my screaming bladder, but Aubrey stopped me with a quick hug. I hugged her back and then she stepped away with another smile and I moved into the bathroom to use the facilities. I decided to go ahead and jump in the shower and the hot water helped...every minute I stood under the hot spray it seemed like I felt a little less hungover. I reluctantly shut the water off feeling a whole lot better than I did when I woke up. I was just about to call out to Aubrey and ask for a towel when I opened the shower door and saw that sitting on the edge of the sink was a stack of clothes and a fresh towel.

I grabbed the towel and quickly dried off and then started going through the clothes. Underwear, sweat pants, a tank top and a sweatshirt. Obviously she wasn't going to loan me a bra (I figured Aubrey had to be at least a DD cup), but how thoughtful was that? I got dressed, choosing to go with just the tank top rather than the bra I wore last night. Everything fit okay if just a little bit too big, but I was super comfy and you were not going to hear me complain.

I emerged clean, comfortable and ready to go to breakfast. Aubrey came over to me with one hand closed and the other holding a bottle of water. I gratefully took the four Advil tablets from her with a tired grin and downed them with half the bottle of water. As soon I finished swallowing, she asked me if I wanted to wear a pair of her ballet shoes or flip-flops.

Hmmm...I tried on the Rainbows and was surprised to find we wore the same size shoe. "These work for me."

"Cool," she nodded as she pulled a polar fleece jacket on over her t-shirt.

We headed out to a little bistro-diner place that was right around the corner from Aubrey's apartment. Twenty minutes later we were a couple of happy girls now that we were elbow deep in eggs, bacon, french toast and coffee. We were not the least bit concerned with manners or looking dainty or lady-like either - at least I wasn't. I was throwing down on all that yummy, greasy goodness, and I think Aubrey was doing a heck of a job of keeping up with me.

Finally stuffed to the brim with all of the fat and carbs we could stand, we both sat back on our respective sides of the booth satiated. From the look on Aubrey's face she was feeling like I was and that meant much better than when we first woke up.

We just kind of sat there for a few moments in a comfortable silence. I was enjoying the last few swallows of what I had decided would be my last cup of the bistro's house-blend when Aubrey cleared her throat. I glanced up to find that she was looking at me with a semi-serious expression on her face like she had something important to say.

I sat up and gave her my full attention.

"I uh, kind of remember saying something last night," Aubrey smiled and then looked down self-consciously. "But I want you to know that I'm truly thankful you were there for me last night."

"I told you last night and I'll tell you again in the light of day, all sober and whatnot," I grinned and then pointed my finger at her like a pistol. "I've got your back, chick."

"No one has ever done anything like that for me before..." Aubrey looked back up at me. "I mean, you stood up to that asshole, and I don't know...it looked like you were willing to get your ass kicked trying to protect me or whatever."

"I don't know about that," I joked. "I think I could have taken him."

"I'm serious, Meghan," Aubrey reached out with a very somber look on her face and placed her hand on top of mine. "I've never known another friend much less a female friend who looked out for me like you do. I want you to know...I really, really appreciate it. And I appreciate you...a lot."

"Back at ya," I smiled and squeezed her hand. "Seriously...I think the world of you. I'm happy we've become such good friends."

Aubrey nodded and then bit her lip, which was like cuter than a whole litter of puppies and I swear it looked like she might start tearing up again. She didn't. Instead, she sat up straight and motioned for the waitress. She insisted on picking up the check. We went back to her place and lounged around on her couch for a while watching reruns of The Walking Dead. I loved spending time with Aubrey...but before long I knew I had to get going. I still had laundry to do if I was going to have anything to wear to work on Monday. We hugged goodbye, but not before I promised that I would definitely come back over to her apartment the next day for Chinese food and more TV time.

I started the drive back to my place and two things suddenly stood out to me. I was in a really good mood and felt like despite all the drama, Friday night and the sleepover and this morning's breakfast had been a lot of fun. I enjoyed all of it immensely...and I kind of missed hanging out with Aubrey already. Was that ridiculous or what? I wasn't even home yet. I found myself smiling in anticipation of tomorrow afternoon. I was actually really looking forward to curling up with Aubrey on her couch and enjoying spring rolls and a movie.

I don't know if I can tell you the exact date and time when it occurred to me, but it wasn't too long after that weekend that I realized Aubrey had become my best friend.

****

After that weekend, there was a noticeable change to my relationship with Aubrey. It was kind of subtle and I don't think I gave it much thought, but Aubrey started treating me differently. I think she felt our friendship was growing into that next level of 'best friendship' and looking back on it now, I don't think she'd ever had like a real female best friend before...not one that she could trust anyways. I'm not going to psychoanalyze it, but Aubrey began to confide in me and ask my advice about pretty much everything.

I of course reciprocated - I loved Aubrey. She was awesome.

I think she also began to really appreciate the fact that I wasn't overwhelmed by her looks and I wasn't about to bow down to her will - I told her the truth and gave her my honest opinion whether she wanted to hear it or not. Aubrey was the kind of person that needed that. Believe it or not, she was actually kind of insecure about a few areas of her life - especially guys. Again, I know it sounds cliché, but it turns out it was true in this case - the prettiest girls don't get asked out all the time because most guys are intimidated by their looks or don't even bother trying. Most of the guys she did end up going out with were pompous assholes that were only concerned with getting into her pants...and I wasn't shy about telling Aubrey that either.

The day started off as just an average day at work - well as average as a Friday can be the week before Thanksgiving. We were both super busy trying to finish up last minute projects and reports on all things marketing before the holiday. I was concentrating on a power point presentation when Aubrey nudged me and gave me that look that I knew meant "follow me." I mentally sighed. It was Friday and I had to finish this presentation before a meeting later that afternoon. I held up a finger so I could finish the slide I was working on. Once I had it done and made one small grammatical correction to it, I proceeded to get up and follow Aubrey out of our little work area and around the corner to the marketing supply room. She ducked into the supply room and dragged me in after her and locked the door behind us.

"Meg, I need your help," Aubrey whispered dramatically and then took a deep breath and let it out slowly as if she was getting ready for an Olympic high dive or something.

"Alright," I shrugged. "What's up?"

"Well...I met this guy," she started to explain, but then stopped and scowled at me when I groaned and rolled my eyes.

"Seriously, Aubs?"

"Yes, seriously," she insisted.

I looked into those expectant amber-brown eyes and finally let out a small sigh as I mentally submitted and prepared myself to try and listen patiently. "Okay, okay...I'm listening."
"I knew I could count on you," Aubrey smiled in relief and then a look of something flashed across that beautiful, flawless face that I'm not sure I had ever seen before.

"What is it?"

"What is what?" she tried to act innocent and I could swear if she wasn't so tan she might have been blushing.

"What's...that?" I clarified by moving my finger in the air in front of her indicating her face. "What's got you acting all shy and embarrassed like...come on, Aubs - spit it out."

"Fine...look," she finally replied and blew out a breath in apparent frustration. "I'm just...I'm like really horny and I haven't had sex in forever and I met this cute guy and you know how I like to do the whole texting tease thing..."

I held my hand out in a calming gesture and spoke slowly since Aubrey had been talking really, really fast. "And?"

"And I know I'm gonna go too far," she whined. She was like the only person I knew who was actually cute when they whined. "I'm like fixin to bust I'm so friggin' horny and I don't want to give away too much in the pics or else...he won't want to go out with me for me or whatever. He'll think I'm too eager and...it'll just be about sex like you're always lecturing me about."

"Okay," I repeated just as slowly. "And?"

"Can you just take the pictures?" she asked and held out her phone to me. "Please?"

I looked from her phone to her half-wincing, half-anticipatory expression and finally sighed. "Fine."

"Thanks, Meg," Aubrey breathed a sigh of relief and after handing me her phone, started to unbutton her shirt. "I knew you'd have my back."

"Yeah...I do," I agreed quietly as I held up her phone and tapped the camera feature and then looked at what she was doing. "Hey, slow down there, hot-to-trot...tease him, remember?"

"Oh...right, right, right," Aubrey mumbled and refastened a couple of her buttons. She pulled on the lapels of her blouse so that her shirt gaped open revealing a pretty beige bra speckled with little white polka dots and lace around the top of the cups.

"Better," I replied as I took a few pictures from different angles. "Cute bra...is that new?"

"It is," she smiled and pulled her shirt open broader so I could get a better look at it...damn, I thought to myself as Aubrey revealed more of her body, this guy has no idea how lucky he is.

"It's too bad you are the proverbial brick house," I advised her as I took the last picture and then held her camera out to her, "because if that fit me I would totally steal your unmentionables."

"I always figured you to be a panty thief," Aubrey cracked.

"I'd only steal your bras," I corrected her. "My panties are way cuter than yours."

"Pishaw!" she scoffed and pulled the waistband of her pants down far enough to expose the top of her panties so that I could see they were part of a set. "I totally match and you know these are damned cute."

"Ah...well, I stand corrected," I announced with my hand over my heart. "Your rump covering is in fact the cutest."

"Thanks," Aubrey smiled and pretended to pull up an imaginary skirt and curtsy. She then batted her eyes which made me giggle.

Suddenly we heard a noise from right outside the supply room door which made me giggle even louder.

"Shhhh," she shushed me and moved closer as if that would make me stop laughing. "You're going to get us busted."

I couldn't help myself as I kept laughing. I'm one of those people that once I get tickled over something, I have a really hard time stopping.

Aubrey shushed me again and put her hand over my mouth and forced me up against the wall. Our eyes met and she was fighting hard not to join me in laughing. I stopped giggling, but not because I got control over myself or because of her efforts...well, actually it was because of her efforts. She had me pinned against the wall with her body and I don't know whether she realized it or not, but her big breasts were pressed up against mine and I could feel how hard her nipples were because they were poking into my boobs.

I suddenly felt really warm and even a bit dizzy as I looked into her eyes.

We just stood there like that for maybe another ten seconds with our bodies pressed together...her face right next to mine...and her hand over my mouth. She finally took her hand away and stepped back with a quiet giggle and started buttoning her shirt back up. "I think the coast is clear."

"Uh-huh," I agreed dumbly as I just stood there against the wall.

"We should probably get back to work."

"Absolutely," I agreed, but still in a daze. "Just so you know - if I get fired for taking titty shots for you, I'm going to be totally pissed."

"You aren't going to get fired," she turned her head and whispered in my ear as she opened the door. She planted a kiss on my cheek and said, "But even if you did - you'd still love me."

And then she was gone, heading back to her work station. I shook my head as I watched her turn the corner and even then a part of me knew that she was right.

****

We had already decided during lunch which restaurant we were going to later that night for dinner and then which club we would hit after that. I finished my project and had just sat down in the conference room with a group of the national sales people when my phone vibrated. Aubrey and I had become like a couple of ninjas when it came to checking our phones and texting during meetings. No one had a clue what we were doing either. We were that good at it.

I surreptitiously looked at my phone in my lap. It was a text from Aubrey. She had attached a couple of the pics from the supply room and wanted me to help her decide which one to send this guy she had been flirting with. I took a long look at both of the pictures and had to admit that they were both smoking hot and seductive. She was just so ridiculously gorgeous. I quickly texted her back and told her which one she should send and I felt...funny. It was kind of weird and I don't think I really wanted to admit it to myself, but I was actually kind of jealous that she was sending seductive pictures of herself to some dude.

I was probably just being over-protective. I put my phone away and refocused my attention on the meeting. My power-point presentation wasn't until the end of the meeting. I felt my phone buzz again. It was Aubrey. Just a quick text asking me if everything was okay...I typed out a quick reply without even looking at my keyboard letting her know I was with a simple 'I'm fine'. She continued to text me asking me if I was upset about something or mad at her to which I kept replying 'no, I'm good'. I finally just had to ignore her and focus on my meeting.

After the meeting she was sitting at her work station looking more than a little unhappy.

As soon as I dumped my laptop, my notepads and file folders on the counter Aubrey turned in her chair before I even had the chance to sit down and asked me what was up. I told her nothing was up as I reconnected my laptop to my docking station. I heard her sigh a little too loudly after I logged in and started checking my email. She scooted her chair over next to mine and damn it, she was wearing Rapture, that Victoria's Secret perfume that smelled so good on her. I quietly took a deep breath of the intoxicating scent of vanilla, amber and just a hint of jasmine and closed my eyes for a second. I finally shook my head. What the hell was wrong with me?

"Why were you ignoring my texts?"

"I wasn't ignoring your texts," I replied as I typed out my response to an email. "I sent you like a thousand texts."

"I know, but..." Aubrey started to argue, but then stopped. I felt rather than saw that she was about to say something else, but then she changed the subject. "So, how did the presentation go?"

"It went well," I smiled and turned my head to look at her. She was giving me a funny look.

"Cool," she smiled back. "So everyone liked it?"

"Yeah," I confirmed as I answered another email. "They're going to go ahead and use my second idea so I've got to start putting together mock-ups."

"Cool," I could see Aubrey nod her head out of the corner of my eye. I continued typing for another minute and then she asked, "What time are you picking me up tonight?"

"Hmmm...the reservation is for eight," I thought out loud, "so I guess...seven fifteen-ish?"

"Sounds good," Aubrey agreed quietly and turned back to her computer.

****

I picked Aubrey up right on schedule.

Well, I didn't really pick her up so much as I parked my car in the lot of her apartment building and I called a cab. That way we could both have fun and not worry about trying to do something stupid like drive under the influence or worry about one of us being the designated driver. I was waiting in the front part of her building when Aubrey glided into view. Wow. She looked absolutely stunning in a simple LBD that really showed off her curves. We hugged and I told her how great she looked and she told me the same.

I thought maybe I was exaggerating in my head about how great Aubrey looked, but she started turning heads as soon as we got out of the taxi. I might as well have been going to dinner with a pin-up girl. I had gone with a more casual teal cocktail mini-dress. Even though Aubrey was the first thing everyone saw, I still managed to get a few appreciative glances which was a nice little ego boost for me. I had to admit we made quite a good-looking couple of twentysomethings out and about for a night on the town. Dinner at our favorite sushi restaurant was spectacular as usual and it seemed like we were both back to our usual friendly selves. I was relieved. Without talking about it we seemed to have gotten past all of our weirdness from earlier in the day.

I had actually given some thought to that weirdness earlier as I was getting ready. I was in the middle of applying my mascara when I came to the conclusion that we were simply in the 'growing pains' stage of our quickly developing best friendship...just silly miscommunications. That's how relationships worked...you continuously learned about each other. There was this weird, vague concern in the back of my mind that we had somehow sort of been acting like a couple earlier. That thought flitted around the edges of my thoughts a few times, but I quickly dismissed it as nonsense. I mean that was silly...we weren't a couple, we were best friends. Right?

After dinner we took another cab to one of Aubrey's favorite bars. The club was crowded and as usual, Aubrey drew a lot of attention. We danced and drank and then two different groups of guys started buying us drinks and shots. It got to the point that I started giving mine away, so it wasn't too big of a surprise that Aubrey ended up getting hammered. I was a little more buzzed than I had intended to get, but still pretty much in control. Wild-child not so much...by the time she wanted to get up and dance on the bar I knew it was time to call it a night.

It was rather chilly as we left the bar from what it was earlier in the evening...but that was the South. This time of year as Thanksgiving and Christmas rolled around we often got forty and even fifty degree temperature swings once the sun went down. We were both shivering as we climbed into the back of the taxi and I gave the driver Aubrey's address. We huddled together for warmth and Aubrey leaned her head on my shoulder and asked me to stay the night at her place. I knew I didn't need to be driving anytime soon, so I agreed. I even had an overnight bag in the trunk of my car. I had kind of figured out that my best friend had an issue with being by herself sometimes and that desire to not be alone tended to get worse when she drank. I didn't mind one bit, though. I loved sleeping over at Aub's and going out for breakfast on Saturday mornings. It had kind of become our thing.

The cab dropped us off and I paid the driver. After a quick detour to grab my overnight bag out of my car, we helped each other up the front steps to the lower-level hallway of her building, shivering, giggling and laughing the whole way. We finally managed to stagger to her apartment, unlock the door and get inside without either of us ending up on our asses. Thank goodness her apartment was nice and warm. We shook off the cold and as per her normal I'm-drunk-routine, Aubrey announced she was taking a shower.

I ignored the trail of clothing she left on her way to the master bathroom and used the guest bathroom to wash my face and brush my teeth. I considered taking my turn in the shower, but gave up on that idea. I was just too tired. I changed into my pj's which consisted of nothing more than a t-shirt and a clean pair of panties. I went into the kitchen and helped myself to a bottle of water out of the fridge. When I got back to the bedroom, Aubrey had the bathroom door open and was standing at the sink brushing her teeth wrapped in a towel.

I took a long drink of water and set the water bottle on the night stand and then climbed into what was basically "my side" of Aubrey's bed. She rinsed and spit and then kind of stumbled over to her side. I was used to Aubrey sleeping in the buff, so it wasn't anything new when she simply dropped her towel and crawled in under the covers beside me. Now just so we're clear -

that didn't mean I didn't appreciate the view. I mean, I think everyone should take the time to appreciate undeniable beauty when the opportunity presented itself.

We squirmed around a bit until I finally ended up flat on my back with my arm under Aubrey's head as she was half turned towards me, half sprawled out across most of the queen-sized mattress. She fidgeted around a bit more and exclaimed "hot" as she pushed the comforter off so that she was only covered with the top sheet. Eventually she settled down and my breathing evened out as I started to relax. My eyes were getting really heavy. I think I was just about to doze off when Aubrey decided in her state of drunkenness that she felt like whisper-chatting.

"Meg," Aubrey staged whispered. "Meggity-Meg."

"What?"

"I gots drunk ta'night," she confided in me and giggled.

"Really?" I mumbled. "Are you sure?"

"Ab-suh-laatool...Ab-sta-loot-tuh..." she declared with each syllable over-pronunciated as she tried so hard to say the word. I felt her shake her head. "Mmyep...I'm sure."

"Then you should go to sleep," I advised quietly with my eyes still closed. "It'll make you feel better."

"Meg," she whispered instead and I could feel her gently poke me in the ribs. "I'm gots drunk, but didn't not get lucky...no luckity duckity."

"I know, hon," I sighed. "Just try to go to sleep now."

"But...it's been suh-long," she whispered-whined.

"Uh-huh," I mumbled with my eyes still closed.

"I...I really need to...y'know," she whispered again after a long pause and didn't sound quite as drunk.

"Uh-huh," I automatically repeated, but didn't move.

"Okay...I'm going to go ahead then..." Aubrey announced quietly and shifted her position slightly, but then seemed to pause again. "Is'at, um... going to bother you?"

I still had a pretty decent buzz going and I was way too tired to move, but Aubrey's words had perked me right up from actually going to sleep. What did she mean 'go ahead then'? Is she talking about masturbating? Is she really going to rub one out right here in bed with me? Seriously? I kept my eyes closed and thought about what she had said...would she really? Maybe she'd go to sleep and this was all just drunk-talk.

Apparently my silent contemplation must have given Aubrey the impression that I'd dozed off...because before I could say anything, I felt her arm closest to me start to move. I peeked my eyes open and wow...okay...there was my best friend lying right next to me with the sheet pushed down to her waist. Nothing too weird about that, except for the fact she slept in the buff...oh, and that she was slowly rubbing and massaging her large breasts. I suddenly felt like I couldn't breathe and realized I was holding my breath. I slowly exhaled as I watched her fingertips slowly trace along the outer contours of her breasts and then she slid her palms up and over to take both of those beautiful, tan globes in her hands. She pushed them together and then gave them a nice squeeze. Damn, she hadn't been kidding - she was going to go ahead and get herself off.

I was kind of fascinated. I'd never watched another girl masturbate before. I just laid there in my faux sleep posture and continued to watch as Aubrey rubbed her unbelievably gorgeous breasts. The thought kind of popped into my head that I really couldn't blame her - I distinctly remembered what those breasts felt like and if I had a pair like that, I'd probably be tempted to play with them too. After a few minutes she switched it up and began toying with her nipples, lightly pinching them and tugging on them. Okay...I guess I had to admit that I was actually more than fascinated, I was utterly freaking captivated. This was probably one of the hottest, most erotic things I'd ever seen. I could feel the flesh of my areolas pucker as my own nipples hardened.

The next thing Aubrey did took me by surprise.

Apparently we had different approaches to our methods of self-love. I had been under the assumption that when I masturbated, I did it, I don't know, kind of normally...but I guess I had never considered - is there really a 'normal'? Up until tonight, I naively thought there was i.e. whenever I did "it" I would lay on my back, play with my tits for a little while and then rub my pussy until I was super turned on. Once I reached the point of being turned on just enough, I would focus on my clit with one hand while I put a finger or two inside myself with the other hand. For me personally, it was a tried and true formula for success. I really don't know why I figured that everyone else - or at least every other woman - must do it pretty much the same way, right?

Yeah...I was wrong.

Aubrey showed me that there could much more to masturbation then simply lying on your back and diddling away. After playing with her breasts, my best friend rolled over onto her stomach. At first she just kind of laid there, gently grinding her hips down into the mattress. She had her head turned away from me so I was given an unobstructed view. I saw one of Aubrey's hands disappear down underneath her and quickly realized that she had to be rubbing her pussy by the way her grinding became more of a humping motion...and it's not like she was just lying on her stomach touching herself. I mean, it was like her whole body was into it. Her legs would change position as her hips moved up and down while her other hand was grabbing the edge of the mattress. It seemed like she was also rubbing her chest against the bed too with the way her upper body undulated.

Damn...I didn't think there was a living soul that wouldn't have agreed that she looked beyond sexy...I couldn't help but start getting turned on myself and I knew my panties were soaked. I was seriously considering sliding a hand down to start playing when Aubrey changed things up again. She brought her knees up so that now she was kind of on all fours, but still had her head down on the bed. I was speechless. With the little night-lite she had over by her bathroom door, I could see her quite clearly. She looked like the word 'erotic' personified. Her knees were spread and her amazing ass was sticking up in the air. I could also see that one of her hands was nestled between her legs. She brought her other hand over and stuck it underneath her upper body so she could grab a handful of one of her boobs. She was gasping and had started to quietly moan as her hips moved and it seemed like she had moved into this kind of zone where she was completely oblivious to me...either that or she didn't care that I was watching her.

Aubrey changed positions again by getting up off of the bed so that she was sitting upright on her knees. I felt my mouth go dry...she was captivatingly beautiful. She was cupping one of her big, round tits with her finger and thumb extended up so she could pull on and pinch her nipple with one hand while the other was buried between her legs. She didn't just sit there either...it was like her body couldn't be still as her hips continued to pump and she flexed her thigh muscles so that her knees slid out a little and then back in with the same rhythm of her pelvis. Maybe the influence of the alcohol was romanticizing this scene, but I felt like I was watching a woman who had totally given herself over to the pleasure she was giving herself. It was like she was fully committed to reaching her climax. There was no subtlety now, no conscious effort not to wake her bedmate...she was well on her way to her peak and would not be denied.

I already said this once, but it's worth saying again because now I knew without a doubt - this was by far the absolute hottest, most erotic thing I had ever seen. I couldn't help but smell

Aubrey's musky, feminine scent and I could definitely hear the distinctively wet, squelching sound of fingers rubbing and fingering wet, slick feminine folds. I found myself with handfuls of sheet balled up in my fists and I was squeezing my thighs together in the same rhythm that Aubrey was moving her hips. She suddenly took her hand off of her tit and reached out to grab the headboard. She used it to steady herself as her ass and hips moved, rocking her body onto the hand that was furiously rubbing her pussy. She tossed her long brown mane back and forth a few times and then she stopped and arched her back.

Aubrey moaned, but she kept her lips together so it came out sounding more like a low humming sound. Her entire body tensed up and then jerked a few times. I could see that her eyes were closed and her pouty lips were curled up in the ghost of a smile. I realized I was tensing up right along with her and I couldn't take my eyes away from her face. I was completely focused on every little expression. I knew she was deep into her rapture and I wanted to soak in every detail from the way her breasts bounced and slightly swayed with every movement to the way she gasped and took in shallow, sharp breaths. Gradually she began to relax and loosened her grip on the headboard. I forced myself to relax my own grip on the sheets.

I kept up my façade of sleep as I watched her with my eyes barely cracked open. I watched Aubrey relax and take a deep, satisfied breath as she sat back on her haunches. I watched her run her hands up the front of her thighs, and on up to cup her breasts briefly and then move so that her arms were wrapped around her body. It looked very much like she literally gave herself a hug. Then I watched her bring the hand that had been deep in her sex to her mouth and she took her time to lick every finger clean, savoring her nectar. She seemed totally relaxed and at peace. Then she silently slid off the bed and disappeared into the bathroom.

I just laid there, my senses overwhelmed. I was awestruck - I had never in my life seen someone give themselves so completely over to pleasure like that. Aubrey seemed totally in tune and in sync with her body in a way that I don't think I had ever experienced. No, check that - I knew for a fact that I had never experienced anything the way Aubrey just had. I closed my eyes and my mind was racing...for a number of reasons. Apparently tonight seemed to be all about new experiences...it wasn't a very big one, but it was definitely a good one.

I had had my own orgasm at the same time Aubrey did without ever even touching myself.

****

We both ended up sleeping in a little later than usual, but our hangovers weren't too hideous. We ate at our favorite place, the same little bistro-diner that we went to every Saturday morning. Breakfast was delicious and after filling our bellies we both felt a lot better. We headed back to Aubrey's place and cuddled under a blanket and binge-watched episodes of Supernatural on Netflix. We giggled and chatted quietly the whole time. It was fun and thoroughly enjoyable. It was our routine and all seemed right in the world.

Except...I couldn't get images of my naked best friend pleasuring herself out of my head. It was like I couldn't even look at Aubrey without my eyes automatically glancing at her generous breasts or her perfectly rounded ass or when I thought she wasn't looking, the crotch of her exercise pants. It was still cold outside, but Aubrey kept the thermostat in her apartment up pretty high so it was actually really warm. So warm that she ran around dressed like it was summer...and the skintight yoga pants and flimsy little tank-top she was wearing sans bra didn't really do a whole lot to discourage my wandering gaze either. What the hell was wrong with me? I think I needed to go home and spend some 'quality time' with myself...I figured if I just gave myself a really good orgasm, I would snap out of it.

After the last episode we were watching ended, I announced that I needed to head home and get some laundry done. It was an excuse, but I actually did need to do a couple of loads...so I didn't feel like I was out-and-out lying. Aubrey protested that she wanted me to stay a little longer. She begged for one more episode, but I held firm. I needed to go. Aubrey decided that if she crawled up on my lap then I wouldn't be able to leave. I tried to escape, so she countered and ended up basically trapping me on the couch by straddling me.

"Do you really have to go?" she asked quietly.

"I do," I sighed and felt terrible for being so selfish...but if I didn't go home and 'take care of business' then I honestly didn't know what would happen.

"You can't stay?" Aubrey pleaded and leaned forward, putting her hands up on the back of the couch and tilting her head down until our foreheads were touching. "Just a little longer?"

"I...uh...okay-okay," I managed to stutter. I glanced down and honestly didn't think Aubrey was aware that by leaning forward she had basically set her large breasts down to rest on the top of my boobs. It didn't seem like a big deal, but I was hyper-aware of the volume and weight of Aubrey's chest touching mine...and the breast to breast contact was making me feel really confused.

I was about to protest, but when I looked up I noticed how close her mouth was to mine. I could feel the blush rising in my cheeks and it wasn't from embarrassment. "I, uh...I'll stay for one more episode."

"Yes!" she exclaimed triumphantly

"On one condition."

"Anything," she smiled excitedly.

"I'll stay if you get off of me," I replied and I really should have stopped to choose my words more carefully, because what I said came out more harshly than I had intended it to.

"Oh," Aubrey flinched and sat up. She immediately pushed up on the back of the couch and quickly got off of my lap. "I'm sorry, I was just...I didn't realize..."

"No, no, no," I shook my head and stood up. I held my arms open and stepped forward to give her a hug. She stiffened for a second as I wrapped my arms around her and I squeezed a little tighter to try and show her I hadn't meant what I said. Wow, the way she felt in my arms was...stop, I mentally chastised myself. I was totally making this creepy. "I apologize, Aubs...I didn't mean it."

"Its fine," she replied over my shoulder and by the tone of her voice I could tell her feelings were hurt.

"Nope, not fine," I corrected and loosened my hug so that I could lean back and look deeply into her eyes. "I sincerely apologize...that was rude and I one hundred percent did not mean it the way it sounded."

At first she wouldn't look at me, but then finally she moved her eyes up. "You really didn't mean it?"

"I swear," I nodded. She was still in my arms in a loose kind of hug. "Forgive me?"

"Okay," she nodded back. "Apology accepted."

"Thank you," I sighed in relief and then pulled her closer for another full-on hug. "I'm just being grouchy."

"Yeah," Aubrey agreed. "That was kind of grouchy."

"I know," I confirmed. "I didn't mean it the way it sounded."

"Did I do something wrong? I was just playing around."

"Nope," I shook my head as I finally ended the embrace. "Not at all...I promise it was all me."

"All you, huh?" Aubrey replied and stepped back to retake her seat on the couch. She pulled her legs up and got comfortable. "What's going on?"

"It's nothing...not a big deal," I tried to downplay it and avoid any further discussion.

"Well, It's obviously a big enough deal to make you snap at me," Aubrey observed with one eyebrow raised. "Come on, talk to me."

"No, it's nothing...seriously," I continued being evasive. I looked over at Aubrey and realized she was looking at me expectantly. "Look...let's just watch the show and then I'll take care of myself..." Wow - did I really just say that? "I mean, I can take care of me..." Okay, I really need to stop talking now. "I'll take care of it...I'll just...take care of it when I get home."

By now both of Aubrey's eyebrows were raised. I could feel how hot my face was with what I knew was a deep crimson blush. I had finally stopped talking and just kind of sat there in all my embarrassment looking sheepishly at Aubrey. I started to wonder if maybe I could still make a break for it when I saw something click in those amber-brown eyes as realization settled on Aubrey's face.

"Meg...wait...is this about last night?" she asked suspiciously and cocked her head. Without waiting for an answer she must have seen the truth in my expression. "It is! Awww...Meg, I'm --"

"NO!" I practically shouted. "I mean, no, its fine...you don't have to explain."

"Meg," Aubrey said my name again and had the most sympathetic look on her face as she scooted across the couch. She moved closer until she was sitting right next to me. She put her arm around my shoulder and she even had her plump lower lip pouted out which was like one of the cutest things I had ever seen in my entire life. "My poor little Meg..."

"Aubrey," I sighed and closed my eyes, using every bit of my self-control not to acknowledge or pay attention to the feel of her heavy breast pressing against my arm. "Seriously...its fine."

"Hey...I totally get it," she moved her shoulders and nudged me and lowered her voice conspiratorially. "How long has it been?"

"How...what?"

"You know," she nudged me again. For Pete's sake, did she even realize she was nudging me with her boob? "Since you got off? Sorry if I was too loud and woke you up or whatever, but I've been in such a dry spell...I just had to do something about it."

"Oh...yeah..." I slowly nodded and then jumped on the chance to play along. "No, pppssht, I get it. I'm with ya, I mean...sometimes you just have to...and, uh...yeah."

"Exactly," Aubrey nodded with a huge grin. "You know, you could have done it, too."

"I'm sorry - could have what?" I asked, but I knew exactly what she meant. I was so confused with everything that was going on in my head that I wasn't really sure how to act.

"You know," Aubrey grinned again and this time when she went to nudge me I turned just a little bit so that her big breast bumped into my breast instead of my arm. Was it immature for me to do that? Very. Cheap thrill? Yep...but did it send goosebumps up and down my arms? Absolutely.

"Oh," I widened my eyes in surprise. "You're saying that last night...I should have - what? Joined you?"

"Well, yeah," Aubrey nodded matter-of-factly. "If you were feeling it I wouldn't have minded one bit. It would have been fun."

I raised my eyebrows in surprise.

"I mean, you're my best friend...I trust you completely," she continued. "I feel like we can tell each other anything, so that means we can, I don't know, do anything together without getting all weirded out about it. Ya know?"

"You really feel that way, Aubs?" I looked at her and for some reason felt like I might cry.

"You know I do," Aubrey's adoring smile practically lit up the room. "You're the dearest and absolute best friend I've ever had...I love you, Meg."

"I love you, too," I smiled and pouted my bottom lip out back at her. How is it possible that her smile seemed to get even brighter as I said that?

Aubrey turned and pulled me into a hug. I hugged her back tightly and I actually felt better. The moment that Aubrey had opened up and said those words, I made a spur of the moment decision to take all of my confused-mixed up-thoughts and just put them away. I forced those odd feelings into a little compartmentalized place in my brain and locked that door. I just didn't want to think about it...not right now.

"I have an idea," Aubrey pulled away and her expression turned into one of excitement. She reached down and grabbed my hand. "Come with me."

****

I got up and let Aubrey drag me down the hall to her bedroom. She led me over to stand by her bed and then told me to close my eyes. I turned around to face her and let out a heavy sigh. "Aubs, what are you doing?"

"Just trust me," she grinned as she flitted about the room. She suddenly stopped and put her hands on her hips. "I thought I told you to close your eyes?"

"Why?"

"Because I asked you to," Aubrey replied stubbornly and just stood there looking at me until I threw my hands up in the air.

"Fine," I closed my eyes. I heard Aubrey giggle in triumph and then some shuffling sounds and a maybe a drawer opening. I was seriously tempted to open my eyes when I heard a scratching sound and immediately smelled the tell-tale aroma of sulfur dioxide. Instead of peeking I stayed true to her request and kept them shut.

"Okay," Aubrey announced and I felt her hands on my shoulders as she gently pushed me backwards until I felt the edge of her bed hit me in the back of my knees and sat down. "Open your eyes."

I opened them to find Aubrey's bedroom lit up in the glow of three strategically placed candles. I caught the slightest hint of gingerbread and caramel in the air. The smells were obviously from the scented candles. Definitely a holiday-ish feel to it, but they were very subtle and I had to admit they did give her bedroom a warm and inviting aroma. Aubrey was standing in front of me, her curvaceous figure dramatically lit by the illumination of the candles. She had the most affectionate, endearing smile on her face.

"Do, you like it?" she asked with what seemed a quiet eagerness.

I nodded my head as I looked around, feeling a little nervous for some reason. "Uh...yeah. I do."

"Awesome," Aubrey's smile grew a little wider. She stepped forward and put her arms around me and gave me another one of her awesome Aubrey-hugs. I instinctively put my arms around her in return and my eyes closed automatically as I enjoyed the sensation of being pulled into all of my best friend's sensuous curves.

Aubrey ended the hug and stepped back and gave me another smile as she brought her hands up to her waist and hooked her thumbs into the waistband of her yoga pants. She slowly started pulling them down and I held my breath. Aubrey hesitated for a moment with the top of her yoga pants pulled down just far enough to reveal the top of her powder blue panties. I couldn't take my eyes off of her hands. Now I honestly don't know if my mind was playing tricks on me or if Aubrey just naturally moved with the sensuality of a professional stripper...but the oh-so-subtle way she slowly wiggled her hips back and forth a few times to get the elastic waistband of her exercise pants over the swell of her hips would have had the stage raining with dollar bills in any gentlemen's club in the world.

After she got the pants over her hips and ass, she continued to peel them down her thighs. She bent over to take them the rest of the way down her legs which gave me an enticing view down her tank top at her generous cleavage. She quite cutely kicked her feet a few times to finally be free of the garment as she straightened back up. She was wearing a really cute pair of lacy boy-short panties that I just now noticed matched her tank-top. I almost chuckled at the fact that her fashion sense was on point even when she was just bumming around her apartment. She had just grabbed the hem of her skimpy top when she stopped and looked at me expectantly.

"What are you waiting for?"

"Huh?" I replied, still in somewhat of a daze. "What am I...what?"

"Get undressed, Meg," Aubrey giggled. "Unless you're seriously planning on leaving your clothes on."

"Um," I was finally paying attention to what was happening right now. "And what are we doing right now?"

"You know," Aubrey nodded her chin and raised her eyebrows. "We're going to do our thing."

"Aubs," I half shrugged my shoulders. "I don't think I exactly understand...what 'thing'?"

Aubrey smiled at me again in some unknown understanding that I apparently wasn't in on. She came over to me and took my hand and then sat down beside me on the bed.

"We're going to do what we should have done last night," Aubrey whispered excitedly. "You know...we're going to masturbate. Together!"

"What?" I asked as the realization hit me about our conversation in the living room and this whole trip to her bedroom. "Aubrey...I...I appreciate it, but no. It's cool. We don't have to do this."

"Meghan," Aubrey continued smiling and held my hand as she cocked her head at me with this knowing look on her face. "I know you need this. I want to...and I know you want to, too."

"Oh, I do, huh?" I replied skeptically.

"Yeah, I think you do," Aubrey confirmed with sincere confidence. "So...just trust me on this one."

I laughed nervously, but she didn't join in. My laughter quickly faded. O-kay...so she really wasn't kidding. I looked down at the floor, blushing like crazy and before I could think of anything else, my mouth went ahead without my authority or written approval or anything and I heard myself say, "Okay..."

"Really?"

"Yeah, I think you're right...and I do trust you."

"Cool," Aubrey smiled. She climbed up further on the bed and I looked up to see what she was doing.

Aubrey had crawled to the middle of the bed and had gotten up on her knees. I immediately flashed back to how incredible she looked last night when she was in that same position touching herself. She grabbed the hem of her tank-top and lifted it up an inch or two, but then stopped as she looked at me. I raised my eyebrows in question.

"Um," she pursed her lips. "It might help if you kind of got naked."

"Oh...right," I nodded and stood up.

I faced the bed as I put my fingertips in the waistband of my sweatpants and nervously pushed them down. They were baggy enough so that they fell down my legs and I stepped out of them as my eyes moved back up and my gaze was immediately glued to Aubrey again. She had crossed her arms and was once again pulling her flimsy shirt up by the hem. I licked my lips in anticipation as that piece of material traveled upwards, revealing first her tan, toned stomach and then a peek at her significant under-boob. She stopped there to check on my progress, so I quickly slid my t-shirt up and off.

I just kind of stood there in my bra and panties as she finished pulling her shirt off. Her large, round breasts bounced slightly as they came free from being covered up by the shirt. My breath caught. I don't think I would ever get used to being this physically close to someone who was as exceedingly beautiful as my best friend...well, at least not when they were in the process of getting naked with the intention of masturbating in front of me. Uh, correction - with me...gulp...I don't think the whole mutual part of this little scenario had quite sunk in for me just yet.

I looked back up into Aubrey's face and the expression she wore stopped me short. Her look was one of expectancy - but not like I would have thought. It was more about the fact that right now she was completely trusting me and her expectation was that I was going to do the same. Yeah, yeah, I know - I'm waxing philosophical when we were fixin to rub our pussies...but I guess you had to be there to understand it. It was deep.

Something clicked. I'm not sure if I can accurately describe what exactly it was that clicked into place in my brain, but I was ready to give myself completely over to what Aubrey wanted. I was ready to commit to this bonding of best friends...to this utterly feminine experience of exploring and touching our bodies to bring ourselves pleasure. Together. I reached my arms up behind my back and shyly returned Aubrey's smile as I unhooked my bra and then slid it off, dropping it on the floor with the rest of my clothes. I climbed up on the bed, still committed to going through with this, but also very self-conscious of my almost naked body in such close proximity to Aubrey's.

I normally don't let myself succumb to such negative, petty comparisons - we as women are all beautiful in our own right. I truly believe that...but trust me, that is a concept that isn't quite as easy to cling to when you suddenly find yourself exposed two feet from a living, breathing centerfold. I was up on my knees in the same position as Aubrey. I covered my much smaller breasts with my hands and kind of looked around the bed, not really sure what to do. Aubrey saved the day and her timing could not have been better.

"Oh, wow," she said earnestly as she looked me up and down. "Meg...you are just so beautiful."

"What?" I giggled nervously.

"I mean you're obviously pretty and have a gorgeous figure and all," Aubrey replied and then shook her head as if in amazement. "But...damn...I had no idea how stunning you would be without your clothes on."

"Seriously?" I arched an eyebrow at her. "The ultimate model for pin-up girl art thinks I'm stunning?"

"Of course," Aubrey looked at me like I was crazy and her tone of voice reaffirmed it. "Meg...wow - just look at yourself." Aubrey emphasized her point by reaching out and gently grabbing both of my wrists and pulled my arms out wide so that I was effectively on display. "I mean, my word, girl - I would kill for your stomach. And your boobs are like...perfect."

I looked down to see if I could actually see what she was talking about. My body was definitely in direct contrast to Aubrey's unbelievable curves. I was more lean and athletic, but I still had curves in all the right places. I think we were going to have to agree to disagree about my boobs - especially compared to hers. But I guess my little six-pack was kind of nice looking...I looked back up and we both smiled and I of course blushed at her comments. Aubrey released my wrists and then we just kind of mutually agreed without actually saying anything to lie down.

We were side by side and I don't think three seconds went by before we both got a case of the giggles.

I'm pretty sure the silliness was a direct result of nervousness, but after we finally got it out of our systems, Aubrey got things started by reaching up and laying her hands on her breasts. She let out a deep sigh and then very slowly began moving her hands as she whispered to me. "This is so exciting."

"Yeah, I guess it is," I agreed and without putting too much thought behind it raised a shaky hand up and let it rest on top of my breast.

"Are you nervous?"

"A little bit," I confessed.

"Nervous is okay...but not scared, right?" She asked and then pulled her legs up until her toes were pointed straight up in the air. She kind of titled her pelvis up for a moment and in one motion stripped off her underwear. She flung them across the room in the general direction of her hamper and then turned her head towards me. She smiled and cocked an eyebrow at me. I knew what that meant.

"No," I replied and pulled my panties off, but with nowhere near as much flair. I leaned over to the edge of the bed and dropped them on the floor in the pile with the rest of my clothes. "I'm not scared...not really. I'm with you, so nothing to be scared of, right?"

"Exactly!" Aubrey's face lit up. She continued smiling at me with her head turned as her hands went back to her breasts. She began rubbing and massaging them more aggressively. "Just do whatever feels good...and enjoy it."

So I did.

Well...at least I tried. As outside of the box of what my expectations were for this Saturday afternoon, you could say that it started off with good intentions. I eventually got over my shyness and started rubbing my breasts and playing with my nipples. It felt good and I knew I was getting wet...but I felt awkward and even though I made a valiant effort not to watch what Aubrey was doing, I really couldn't help myself...but can you blame me? So what started out as "normal" (there's that blasted word again) - turned into Aubrey and I touching ourselves as we watched each other.

Nothing was said or planned or anything like that...things just kind of escalated. As soon as Aubrey really got going, she just did what Aubrey does when she got into it - which is she moved around, changed positions and got up on her knees again only this time she was facing me. She motivated me to move around as well. I basically just mirrored everything she did. We both ended up on our knees, our hands on our pussies, rubbing, fingering, tasting our nectar...on a side note I had never done that before, but she did it like literally right in front of my face and I felt compelled to follow her lead. Wise decision on my part - I loved it.

When we reached our orgasms it was almost at the same time, but she beat me to the punch by about ten seconds. When she came, she instinctively reached out to steady herself and ended up using my shoulder to brace against. This brought our bodies really, really close together. We didn't physically touch other than her hand on my shoulder, but her heaving breasts were like less than an inch from mine and her face right there in front of me. It was amazing.

I have to confess, watching Aubrey from such an extremely close vantage point as she orgasmed was over-the-top exciting...I mean seeing the little nuances of the look on her face and being able to witness the way her body trembled and moved during her orgasm was nothing short of spectacularly beautiful...but when she touched me? When her hand physically made contact with my skin? That was what drove me over the edge. It was the strongest orgasm of my life.

Watching Aubrey cum and then knowing she was watching me while I came? I realized that this trumped the other experience and had now officially become the new, absolute hottest thing that had ever happened to me or that I had ever been a part of...and it made me cum again.

****

Of course our relationship changed again after that weekend...for the better.

We were now unconditionally the bestest of friends. The more we hung out and got to know each other on different levels, more intimate levels, the more I came to love and admire Aubrey. What was not to love? I mean, she was funny, smart, witty, silly and of course drop-dead gorgeous. I found myself enjoying the time we spent together more than I have ever enjoyed being around another human being.

Of course Thanksgiving meant spending time with our families, but we did it together. Half the day was spent with Aubrey's family which was wild and crazy with all of her aunts and uncles and cousins. The food was ridiculous and I had a blast listening to all of their stories about when Aubrey was little. We played board games and ate until we couldn't move. It was so enjoyable and we had the absolute best time. I loved her family.

My family on the other hand was much smaller since I didn't have as many extended relatives. Since it was normally just me and my parents, we usually didn't make that big of a deal out of Thanksgiving. Not like Aubrey's family did...but I had promised my mother we'd be there. I was actually kind of excited when I found out we would have a special guest this year. I really wanted Aubrey to meet one of my favorite people in the whole wide world, my Auntie Kate. So we left her parent's house and spent the rest of the day with my family.

Auntie Kate often traveled during the holidays, but this year she was spending both Thanksgiving and Christmas with us. She was actually my mom's Aunt so technically she was my Great Aunt, but I called her Auntie Kate anyways. She was like the coolest, most fun person I knew and ever since I was a teenager I felt like I could always confide in her without judgement. I seriously didn't even know how old she was. She wouldn't say and she certainly didn't look or act like she was in her seventies which I knew she had to be. I just respected and loved her so much and was so excited to introduce her to Aubrey.

I was actually pleasantly surprised at the spread my Mom put on. I had the feeling Auntie Kate probably had a hand or two in making sure the menu was up to snuff. Either way, the two of them went to a lot of trouble so of course we both felt obligated to eat again. I even had seconds of dessert at my Auntie's insistence. The food was great and afterwards my dad made a fire in the fireplace. We just kind of sat around and chatted. Both of my parents seemed to like Aubrey well enough and I could tell Auntie Kate just loved her to pieces. It made the whole day so much fun. With Auntie Kate here it was the first time in quite a few years I actually enjoyed Thanksgiving. It even made me start to look forward to Christmas.

Aubrey seemed to be having the time of her life. I studied her when she wasn't looking. This was all sort of new to her since she'd never had a real best friend before. To be honest, this felt pretty new to me too since I had never been as close to anyone as I was to Aubrey. The more I looked at my best friend, the more it sunk in that her being happy made me happy. I guess this is what it meant to really love someone...as a friend of course.

As weird as this may sound, but being Aubrey's best friend and Aubrey being Aubrey also meant that masturbating together was not a one-time thing. The second time it happened was that same holiday weekend. Somehow I let her talk me into going shopping on Black Friday...a first for me and I still rue that decision. Later on after a well-deserved nap, we went out to dinner and then stopped by a club where we both got tipsy. We had a lot of fun dancing, drinking and just talking to people. It was kind of funny that when we finally decided to call it a night, we took a cab back to Aubrey's apartment for our weekly sleepover without even discussing it. I guess we both just assumed that that was the plan.

Again, we did our routine thing with Aubrey taking her quick shower. Neither of us felt like watching TV, so we just decided to go to bed. I wasn't going to say anything or bring it up, but in the back of my mind I was definitely curious to see if...maybe? Yeah, there was no maybe involved as Aubrey initiated it as we were getting ready for bed. She just threw it out there like it was no big deal: Hey, so do you want to get off with me? Of course I did. I wasn't nearly as hesitant or shy this time around thanks to the alcohol, but it still felt surreal. I suppose I felt just a little bit awkward at first, but once we were both naked, it was game on.

It was also just as blazing hot as the first time and we both came really hard.

The third time actually happened the following morning...but ended up being a little different. We slept in and just kind of lounged around in Aubrey's bed for a while, chatting about nothing really. I had finally let Aubrey talk me into skipping the whole pajama thing like she did and I had to admit sleeping naked felt incredible. I wasn't sure what was better - the feel of clean, cool sheets against my skin when I first got in bed or the luxurious warmth of waking up warm and naked under the covers first thing in the morning. Either way - I was now a firm supporter of slumbering in the buff.

Anyways...it was Saturday morning. We were lazing about in Aubrey's bed trying to work up the motivation to physically get up and take showers so we could hit our favorite little place for a late breakfast. The only problem was the temperature had dropped overnight and between the warmth of Aubrey's fluffy comforter and our cozy little den of body heat under the covers, neither one of us really felt like moving. I had just worked up the fortitude to jump up and make a naked dash for the bathroom when Aubrey put her arms above her head in a big yawn and a stretch that ended in a giggle.

"What?" I turned my head.

"Mmmm," Aubrey stretched again, only this time she didn't end the stretch in a giggle. She ended it by pushing the blanket and sheet down and cupping her breasts as she purred, "I'm still horny."

"Is that right?"

"Mmmhmm," she blinked at me as her right hand left her breast and eased its way over her stomach until it disappeared under the sheet. I saw the lump under the blanket start slowly moving right at the point where I guesstimated her vagina would be.

"Alrighty then," I chuckled. "Well, you do your thing while I take a shower."

"Awww," Aubrey gave me a sad face, but then grinned. "Come on...do it with me."

"I, uh..." I started to say, but then Aubrey closed her eyes in obvious pleasure and I glanced down. I couldn't help but watch the way she was softly rolling her nipple between her thumb and finger. Her other hand was still moving under the blankets.

"Please?" Aubrey's eyes were still closed, but she was pouting her bottom lip out.

If she would have opened them she would have seen that she didn't have to beg. I had already laid back and had my hands on my breasts. I gently started rubbing and kneading my modest boobs and then took my very erect nipples in between my fingers and was able to squeeze both of them at the same time while still massaging my breasts. Aubrey opened her eyes and watched me for a moment with a big smile on her face.

I closed my eyes and let my right hand wander down the flat of my stomach until I was lightly cupping my mound. I knew I was already wet. I could smell Aubrey's musky sweet scent and it only turned me on even more. I opened my eyes and found Aubrey looking back at me through a heavy lidded squint. She arched her back a little and by doing so changed her position in that she moved closer to me. Our shoulders were actually touching as she settled back into her pillow. I could feel the tiny little vibrations of the movements of her hand on her pussy through that skin to skin contact. I couldn't help myself as I let out a moan and ran my fingers down through my trimmed pubic hair to touch my labia.

"Mmm...fuck yes," Aubrey whispered to me in response to my moan.

"Uh-huh," I agreed as I wiggled my finger to part my swollen inner lips. I shuddered as I dipped the tip of my finger into just the entrance of my slippery core and then traced that finger back up to my clit. I teased myself with just the softest touch on my pearl and had to bite my lip.

Our movements had caused the sheet to move down until it was bunched up around our knees. We were both completely exposed to each other...and we weren't being shy about out-and-out looking at each other, either. I couldn't help but notice that Aubrey was much more relaxed and subdued. It wasn't that she wasn't enjoying herself - her moans and groans made it pretty obvious that she was. It just seemed like she was making this more about us this time rather than just getting herself off.

This morning felt different...there was a feeling of intimacy between us.

Yeah, this time was definitely different...but not a bad different at all. It just seemed like this was the first time we were being deliberate...we were intentionally masturbating for each other rather than two girls who happened to be masturbating at the same time. We were watching each other...almost performing for each other...and I don't know, just enjoying each other. It made it that much more exciting. I know for me, it was a huge turn on lying so close to Aubrey as we touched ourselves. Our shoulders and now our upper arms were in constant contact and it felt...whew, just so fucking hot. The occasional wave of pleasure would make my eyes close for a moment or two, but I tried to keep them open so that I could continue to watch Aubrey play with her breasts and rub her pussy.

I was just starting to ride the outer edge of my orgasm when I switched from my right to my left hand. I was really starting to feel it and it was going to be a big one. I had just finished sucking my nectar off of my fingers and had put my right hand down by my side to rest it for a minute. Without a word Aubrey took her hand off of her breast and reached down. She grabbed my hand and adjusted hers so that our fingers were intertwined as she started to gasp.

"I'm...I'm...so close, Meg."

"Yes," I encouraged her and wondered where I had suddenly found my voice. I'm guessing my newfound courage could easily be attributed to endorphins because I was really, really turned on. I decided to just go with it. I squeezed Aubrey's hand as I rubbed my clit faster. "Yes...cum for me, Aubs. Cum for me."

"Uh-huh...uh-huh," she gasped her agreement and turned her head towards me. Her face had a look of utter concentration on it and her hand was a blur.

"Cum for me, baby," I whispered.

That request seemed to do it for her...Aubrey's lips parted and she kind of let out this quiet moan as she lifted her hips up slightly. Her muscles seemed to go rigid as she held that position, her hand still moving on her pussy as her legs and breasts began to quiver with her spasms. She suddenly dropped her hips to the bed as her breathing came in shallow gasps and then she went rigid again and lifted her hips back up almost towards me like she wanted me to really see her. After what seemed like a really long time, but was probably only about ten seconds, she collapsed back onto the bed with her eyes closed and her large chest heaving up and down. I continued to hold her hand as I watched her every movement.

My fingers made faster and faster circular motions around my swollen clit. I was lost in my own efforts when Aubrey opened her eyes and whispered, "Are you close?"

The sound of her voice was the last little push I needed.

I nodded my head and then boom-shaka-laka. My whole body shuddered and I moaned loudly as my orgasm rocketed through me. My muscles clenched and then released as fireworks went off somewhere deep inside of me. The pleasure was unreal as it seemed to continue longer than usual, rolling over me in what felt like waves, one after another. I turned towards Aubrey and curled up on my side into the fetal position as the throbs of pleasure finally started to decrease in intensity. I didn't even realize how close I was to Aubrey as a result of rolling over or that I was still holding her hand as little aftershocks made my legs twitch and jump.

"Wow!" Aubrey whispered excitedly into my face. She had mimicked me by rolling on to her side towards me and was running her hand soothingly up and down my back. "That must have been a good one."

"Uh-huh," I mumbled and felt numb all over...but I wasn't numb enough that I didn't feel Aubrey's body against mine. We were practically touching from head to toe. I opened my eyes when Aubrey put her free arm around me. She rested her face right beside mine so that we were literally cheek to cheek. I became aware of the weight of her heavy breasts pressed right up against mine. I closed my eyes and put my free arm around her waist and just let myself linger in the warmth of her skin touching mine and her scent in my nose. She smelled wonderful.
She finally ended the embrace by kissing my cheek and rolling on to her back with a sigh. I couldn't help but marvel once again at just how perfect her big breasts were...or how the sun streaming in from the cracks in the blinds lit up her face in profile, highlighting just how beautiful she was. I felt the sudden urge to do something, but the spell broke when she yawned and sat up. She stretched out her arms and then moved her head around to work out some kinks in her neck. I hadn't moved yet...hell, after that climax I wasn't really sure I could. Aubrey

stood up and announced that she was starving and sashayed her way to the bathroom.

I'm not really sure that I was even aware that my eyes were following her every move until she disappeared behind the bathroom door.

****

It didn't take me long to figure out that the month of December was the slowest time of the year for my new company.

Slow as in not a lot to do...as in not enough work to pass the time...as in bored to tears. For some reason the closer the calendar crawled towards the Christmas holiday, the slower it got. In fact, quite a few of the veteran employees saved their vacation days so that they could take the whole week or even two weeks off for Christmas. Being that I had only been here for a couple of months, I of course didn't' have any vacation time banked yet. The company did give all of its employees Christmas Eve day, Christmas day and the day after Christmas off as paid holidays so that was something to look forward to. In the meantime I was stuck having to go to the office every day. Aubrey had used up most of her vacation on a beach trip over the summer, so at least I wasn't lonely.

At first not having a lot to do drove me crazy with boredom especially with how quiet our part of the building was since well over half of our department including the Director were on vacation. Lucky for me this wasn't Aubrey's first rodeo, so even though we might not have been work-busy...we managed to entertain ourselves by texting each other, playing games, watching videos and just hanging out. I guess it was kind of nice to goof off a little, but I should have figured that Candy Crush and YouTube would only go so far before my best friend's inner 'wild child' decided to show up.

I was lounged back in my chair trying to get to the next level of some mindless game on my phone when the icon popped up in the corner indicating I had a new text. I paused my game and opened the message. Of course it was from Aubrey. Follow me right quick. I turned my head to look at her, but she was already up and walking away. With a shrug and nothing else better to do I got up and followed her.

We ended up in our favorite little hidey hole - the Marketing Department's supply room.

I shut the door behind me and turned to Aubrey and whispered, "What's up?"

"I'm freakin' bored," Aubrey announced. She looked really cute today. She was wearing this form-fitting dress that was made to look like a long sweater with buttons all the way up the front. It really showed off her curves.

"Okay," I smirked. "Join the club."

"And I'm horny," she grinned and began to slowly unbutton the front of her dress.

"Oh, great," I sighed. "So I get to play lookout?"

"Nope," she shook her head and took a step closer to me. She stopped what she was doing and reached out her hands and unbuttoned the top button of my long sleeved blouse.

"Um," I gulped and looked down at her hands. "What...are, uh...what are we doing right now?"

"Come on," Aubrey whispered and bit her bottom lip as she unbuttoned the next button of my shirt. "This will be fun...and really hot."

The marketing storage room had two light switches, one for each row of fluorescent lights. Aubrey took her hands off of my blouse and reached over and flipped one of the switches. The row of lights directly above us went out so that we were now partially cast in shadow. Aubrey's hands went back to her sweater dress and unbuttoned another button. I watched in anticipation as the now dramatic lighting cast some incredible shadows on her generous cleavage. The next button undone revealed the center part of her bra. Aubrey paused at the next button and looked up at me with that cute little grin of hers.

"Do it with me...please, Meg?"

"Fine," I sighed and rolled my eyes as my fingers fumbled with the next button on my shirt. "Why in the world I let you talk me into this stuff, I'll never know."

"Cause I'm your best friend and you love me," Aubrey giggled quietly and after unfastening the last of her buttons pushed the front of her dress apart.

"Oh, wow...I love those!" I exclaimed. I couldn't take my eyes off the bra and panty set she was wearing. It had to be new as I'd never seen it before...okay, I guess I have to admit I wasn't so much captivated by the bra or the matching panties so much as what they were covering. "Where did you get them?"

"They're Wacoal," Aubrey replied and looked down at her bra. She slowly ran her hands over the sheer, lacy cups of the peach colored bra. She looked back up at me. "I bought them online. You really like them?"

"They're super cute," I murmured as I watched her hands continue to move along the outside of her large breasts. My shirt was completely unbuttoned and I glanced down to see my own hands moving up my rib cage to lightly stroke the underside of my simple black bra as if they had minds of their own.

"You should check out the website," Aubrey's voice was just above a whisper as she took a step towards me. She ran her hands down her stomach and then along the waistband of her matching panties. "They have really good prices."

"They do?" I asked quietly as she took another step closer to me. Her right hand had moved down so that she was cupping her mound while the other hand had moved back up to squeeze one of her breasts. I unbuttoned my pants and put my hand down the front of them so that I could mirror her actions. The gusset of my panties was already soaking wet.

"Mmmhmm," Aubrey nodded and then pulled the cups of her bra down, first one and then the other so that her ample breasts were exposed. I did the same and my nipples were painfully hard. Aubrey lifted her hand up off of her sex so that she could slide it down her stomach and inside of the waistband of her panties. I followed her lead and exposed my breasts before slipping my hand inside my panties. Aubrey moved just a little closer so that she was standing right in front of me. "I got them...for...sixty percent off."

"Oh, wow," I groaned as my fingers slid down through my trimmed hair and I gently pressed them against my labia. I pushed my hand further down so that I could draw my middle finger upwards to part my swollen inner lips. My hand was already drenched with my slippery juices as I ran my fingertips slowly up and down my slit. "That sounds like a really great deal."

"It...was," Aubrey panted. She removed her hand from her pussy and popped her fingers into her mouth to taste herself. I couldn't help but moan since she was standing close enough that I got a very good whiff of her scent. Her hand went right back to her pussy and I looked down as her other hand began pinching and pulling on her rock-hard nipple.

My hand moved up and I did the same to my breast. I watched her fingers gently tug on her nipple...her nipple that was only about three inches away from my nipple. I watched in slow motion as her hard little summit moved forward and then it was lightly touching my boob. I could feel the rubbery texture of it against the sensitive inside curve of my breast as my eyes shot up. I looked directly at Aubrey who was now leaning in toward me. Both of her exposed breasts pressed up against mine...which also happened to mean that her right breast was not only pressed up against my breast but it was also pushed up against my left hand that was still on my breast. Aubrey's breast felt warm and heavy against the back of my hand.

I nervously licked my lips as her face got closer and closer to mine and... Wait...was she about to...was she going to kiss me? Aubrey continued leaning in and then her face bypassed mine to the side until she could whisper in my ear.

"I think we should try and do it together this time."

"You do?" I croaked as she continued leaning in against me so she could maintain her whisper-in-my-ear position. My head was spinning and I felt like I couldn't do anything but just stand there. Aubrey was close enough that the back of her hand that was rubbing her pussy was starting to bump against the back of my hand that was doing the same thing.

"Yes," she hissed softly. "I think it would be really hot...if we came at the same time."

"Okay," I managed to whisper.

She moved her head back a little and gently rested her forehead against mine. Her eyes were closed, but I know she had to realize that our breasts were still touching and our hands kept making contact. I could feel her hand start to move faster and she let out a little moan.

"Are you close?" she asked in a raspy voice. She began to slowly move her hips which caused her body to shift and her nipples to scrape against mine.

"Uh-huh," I mumbled through a small groan. I had been on the verge of losing it as soon as our boobs touched the first time...now I was practically bursting.

"Me too," Aubrey murmured and reached up and grabbed the shelf above my head with her left hand which pushed her body more firmly against mine. She still had her eyes closed. She was breathing heavier and I could feel the movements of her hand pick up even more speed. Her heavy breasts were now rubbing up and down against mine. "Are...are you ready?"

"Uh-huh," I gasped and realized that I had started to move too. I was not only rubbing my clit, but I was basically grinding my body against Aubrey's.

"Cumming!" she cried out in a short, quiet bark of a voice and tensed up with her body pressed up against mine. I immediately felt my own orgasm start to course through me and I pushed my hips forward so that our masturbation hands were so close together it was hard to know where hers started and mine stopped. Our bodies were touching from our thighs to our tits and I honestly couldn't tell which shivers and trembles were mine and which ones were Aubrey's. I suddenly felt Aubrey kind of sag against me. It was the change in her posture that caused my mind to fully grasp the fact that while we were cumming, my hand had shifted from squeezing my own breast and had been firmly grasping and massaging Aubrey's boob.

"Holy...fuck!" Aubrey panted as she lifted her arms up to hug me. I moved my arms, one hand moving off of my pussy and the other letting go of Aubrey's breast, and hugged her in return. I was quite cognizant of our barely dressed bodies pulled together tightly by the hug. The contact of our breasts pressed together and our hips touching was only making me feel even more confused...I could not deny how incredible Aubrey felt in my arms.

"Agreed," I breathed. My back was beginning to hurt from leaning on the shelves behind me, so I pushed my body forward a little.

"Thank you," Aubrey whispered into my ear with that cute little giggle of hers. She kissed me on the cheek and stepped back effectively ending the embrace.

I just kind of stood there for a moment with my shirt unbuttoned, my bra cups pushed down and only now became aware that my slacks had fallen down around my knees. I watched as my best friend adjusted her bra and began refastening the buttons on the front of her dress. I came out of my daze and pulled up my slacks and got my clothing situated. We stepped to the door of the storage room together and then took one last pause to make sure our clothing was straightened up and we both looked presentable. Aubrey grinned at me and I smiled back.

"I think that was the best one yet," she nodded confidently and winked at me right before she opened the door.

I completely agreed.

****

I walked around in a very confused haze for the next couple of hours. What just happened? At one point Aubrey even asked me if I was feeling alright or if something was wrong. I put on my happy face and explained it away as just a small head-ache. Aubrey was acting normal. Totally normal like what had happened in the storage closet was just not a big deal...so...I decided I would to. She acted like that was just typical behavior for best friends...so I decided I'd act that way as well. Overall, Aubrey seemed to be in a really good mood. I took all of my confused feelings and stuffed them into what I now imagined was this closet in my head. Hmph. I had a hard time mentally closing that imaginary door - the closet seemed to be getting kind of full...but I did it and forced myself to be in a good mood.

The rest of the week was just boring work stuff, but then Friday finally rolled around. We went out and took a long lunch. We ate slices of pizza and then stopped by the mall that was down the street from work so we could do a little Christmas shopping. It was fun. At one point as we strolled in front of all the decorated shops I came to the realization that I was completely at ease and comfortable around Aubrey. Like comfortable in a way I don't think I had ever been before. Huh...in fact I couldn't think of one other person I'd rather spend time with. I shook off those thoughts as we chatted and made plans to go out later.

I drove over to Aubrey's apartment complex and then we took a cab to this Italian place we'd heard about. If it was even the least bit possible, I swear I would have packed up all of my stuff and moved in with that lasagna. It was that good. I had never tasted anything that delicious in my entire life. Aubrey had the chicken picatta and while there is no doubt whatsoever that it was scrumptious - it didn't stand a chance against how good my lasagna was. We also shared a bottle of wine and by the time we left the restaurant to go to the bar I think we were both on our way to being a little tipsy.

The bar was crazy crowded and the entire place was of course all decked out in Christmas decorations. We saw some people we knew as regulars and had a drink with them. It was raucous and fun, but after a few more shots and an hour of being groped and jostled on the dance floor I was ready to call it a night. Aubrey wanted to stay, so of course I waited on her. She danced and drank. She was being really flirty and guys were buying her shots left and right. I was drunker than I usually allow myself to get, so I knew Aubrey was headed to sloppy drunk any shot now. I finally decided enough was enough and managed to corral her and help her outside. We grabbed a taxi and headed back to her apartment.

Physically getting from the cab to her apartment was a little more difficult than usual, but we managed to make it inside without any falls or puking incidents. Aubrey did her usual thing of heading straight to the shower leaving the usual wake of scattered clothes as she started undressing as soon as her front door closed. I followed after her and picked them up and tossed them into her hamper as her naked self shut the bathroom door. I shook my head with a smile as I got undressed and crawled under the covers of Aubrey's bed. I guess I was still buzzing pretty hard because I fell asleep flat on my back as soon as my head hit the pillow.

"Meg," Aubrey whispered.

"What?" I croaked. I finally got one of my eyelids to cooperate and it opened a crack. Aubrey was leaning over me with a big silly smile on her face.

"Are you tired, sleepy-head?" Aubrey giggled and then tickled me in my ribs. It's funny, but the fact we were both naked didn't even seem like a big deal now that I was used to it.

"Me?" I said louder this time as I cringed away from her. I was very ticklish and she knew it. "Why would you think that?"

"Are you too tired to play?" Aubrey whispered and giggled again.

"I'm up," I grumble-mumbled, but closed my eyes again.

"Awwww," Aubrey pouted and I felt her hand lightly tickle its way up over my ribs and briefly touched the underside of my boob as she tried to wiggle her fingers under my arm. "You're gonna miss all the fun."

"Mmph...I'm up," I replied, but I don't think my lips even moved.

I could tell that Aubrey was on her side facing me. I cracked my eye back open and she was lying there propped up on her elbow. Her free hand was making a circuitous route of her body...her fingertips lightly running down her side and over her hip and then back up to trace the contour of each of those lovely large orbs. She had this little smile on her face as if she was just exploring her own body and was pleased with what she discovered. I couldn't fault her there. In the dim light cast by her night-lite, she looked breathtaking. Her long chestnut hair was pushed back to flow down and over her shoulder. Her flawless, tanned skin looked almost bronze in the shadows. I opened my other eye and visually followed her hand over the luscious curve of her hip and up to the swell of her breasts that were perfectly accentuated by her trim waist.

My goodness, but my best friend was beautiful.

I was getting excited so I brought my hands up and let my fingertips dance around my chest. They touched the outer sweep of my breasts and then I ran my fingers down to the sensitive underside of my boobs. I lingered there at the pleasurable sensations that gave me. I let my hands sweep up to run lightly up and down the modest valley between my breasts. My fingers move outward in a circular motion to kind of trace the outline of my boobs in opposite directions at the same time. My fingertip route grew smaller until just the very tips of my fingers were circling my areolas. They puckered and hardened at the attention and I could feel my nipples swell. Aubrey had been watching me intently.

"I'm glad you decided to join me," she had leaned right over me to bring her lips to my ear and it once again brought our bodies into contact. Her heavy bosom rested on my right breast and shoulder as she paused after her whisper and I could almost swear I thought I felt her kiss the side of my neck.

"Well, I couldn't let you have all the fun," I whispered with a grin as I brought my hands down to rub up and down my stomach.

"I really think..." Aubrey pulled her head back to look me in the face as she whispered...but she didn't move her body off of me. She was still kind of on her side but leaning against me as she reached her hand down between her legs. I could feel her thigh pressed firmly up against mine and the side of her hand was rubbing against my hip as she began to slowly move it up and down her sex. "...that we should do it again."

"Do what?" I asked and my mouth suddenly felt dry.

"You know...this," Aubrey replied as her hips began slowly undulating which caused her breasts to rub back and forth against my shoulder and boob a little bit. "So we can cum together like we did at work. Okay?"

"Okay," I immediately agreed without even thinking about it. I was so completely turned on right now that I was one hundred percent committed to doing whatever she wanted without question. My hand was on my pussy, but I was just lightly running my fingers up and down my slit, teasing myself. I was trying to hold off, waiting for Aubrey to let me know when she was close...because I swear the moment I touched my clit I was just going to explode right then and there.

"Damn, Meg," Aubrey moaned and pushed her hips forward so that it forced her hand to be trapped between my hip bone and her pussy. She sort of started to grind on me - well, grind on her hand but with my assistance if that makes sense. She then purposely moved her shoulders to rub her breasts back and forth against me since she didn't have a free hand to touch them. "Doing this...together...is just such a huge fucking turn on, isn't it?"

"Absolutely," I agreed quietly and found myself pushing my chest kind of towards Aubrey so that her breasts were really rubbing up against me.

"It...feels so good," Aubrey announced before she suddenly switched positions and laid down flat on her back right next to me. She scooted over so that from head to toe our bodies were touching on the side closest to each other. I was a little disappointed that she wasn't rubbing her breasts against me anymore, but then a huge thrill ran up my spine when she picked up the leg closest to me and draped it over mine.

"Aubs, are you getting close?" I gasped and forced my hand to stop moving on my pussy before I lost it. I could feel my heartbeat pulsing through my slick lips as my fingers stopped moving.

"Mmmhmm, I am," Aubrey was breathing hard now too. I could see her fingers working her clit and thought the wet little sounds were just as sexy as hell. I glanced down and saw that she was reaching for my hand, but my right hand was kind of occupied. I felt her fingers trace down my arm as she continued rubbing her pussy and then she moaned and her hand gripped the very top of my thigh...the spot on my leg that was dangerously close to my pussy.

"Cumming...I'm...cumming," Aubrey announced through clenched teeth and I could feel her body almost begin to vibrate. Her hand gripped my leg tighter so that her knuckles were touching my hand as I rubbed my clit. "Meg! Cum with me..."

"Yes...YES!" I told her and my voice trailed off as my orgasm bubbled over my consciousness.

I remember my eyes closed. I remember how good Aubrey felt against me as she came. I also remember that I felt a sudden surge of electric pleasure emanate from my clit. It felt so unbelievably good that it was almost painful as that pleasure jolted what seemed like every nerve ending in my body...and that's about all I remember. I mean, it was a truly mind-bending, off-the-chart orgasm...so big that I guess I sort of blacked out for a little while.

I finally opened my eyes and found myself looking directly into Aubrey's. We were lying on our sides facing each other like before. She had scooted up so that we were sharing a pillow. Her flawless face was just right there in front of me about six inches away. I was suddenly a little embarrassed and didn't know whether to smile or cry or what, but suddenly Aubrey's infectious grin was lighting up her face and I couldn't help but smile back at her.

"Holy shit!" she squealed excitedly and put her arm around me. "That was fucking awesome!"

I could only nod as speech seemed to allude me.

She leaned on me and cuddled into me with a hug so that she was practically lying on top of me. It was like she was trying to get as physically close to me as she possibly could. My mind was overwhelmed with sensations. Her large breasts were pressed tightly against my chest and I could feel her hard nipples poking into my breasts. She had instinctively shifted her legs to fit close to me which made our thighs go in between each other's legs. I not only felt her wetness on top of my thigh, but I could feel the soft folds of her pussy against it, too...and I was all too aware that my own still very wet sex was pressed directly against her thigh as well. I felt a funny butterfly kind of feeling in the pit of my stomach.

I honestly don't know who moved first or exactly how it started...but somehow, some way we both started to slowly hump ourselves against each other's thighs. Neither of us said a word to each other. We were still hugging each other tightly. My face was kind of in between Aubrey's head and her shoulder that she was lying on and Aubrey had her face buried in the burrow of my neck. Her lips were close to my ear and I could hear her breathing grow heavier as I felt her pussy move against my thigh.

It didn't take long for either of us to pick up the tempo. I mean it didn't take long at all before we were really thrusting and pumping our hips, grinding away against each other's thighs. This was so confusing to me...this was beyond masturbating and feeling good together, but I've never been more turned on in my life. I could feel her juices running down my leg and I knew I was just as wet. We were both starting to gasp and had worked up a sweat so that our chests were slick with perspiration. The movement of our bodies was causing this really pleasant warm friction as our breasts rubbed together.

I could hear Aubrey whimpering in my ear and then she was whispering to me. "I'm close...I'm close...cum with me, Meg. Please...cum with me."

It was almost magical. Aubrey started to cum with her pussy firmly planted against my thigh and mine against hers, our upper bodies hugging tightly and then my orgasm began right on the heels of hers. We shook and grasped to hold each other tighter as we came, panting into each other's neck. To gain a better purchase in our embrace I felt her hand slide down my back and firmly grab my ass cheek. It felt amazing and extended my orgasm even longer. My mind was kind of reeling as I really didn't know what to think...but without a doubt I've never felt closer to someone. We both finally just kind of collapsed in a loose embrace, our bodies twitching slightly with the little aftershocks of our orgasms.

I was really glad when she finally broke the silence because I didn't' have the first clue as to what to say after something like that.

"I just love you so much," Aubrey whispered and leaned back from our intimate embrace to give me the most genuine smile of affection. She leaned forward and softly pressed her lips against mine in a brief, soft kiss and then pulled back again with a satisfied sigh as she added, "my best friend."

I was once again speechless, but managed to smile at her. The last thing I remember was snuggling into each other as we fell asleep.

****

Ugh. The one and only thing I wanted to know was how in the hell did Monday get here so fast?

I trudged my way through the almost empty parking lot, keeping my head down against the cold. The temperature had taken a serious nosedive last night and I was freezing. I scanned my key card to unlock the door and then wearily walked up the flight of stairs to the second floor. I knew there were only three days until the 24th and even though I was really looking forward to a five day weekend, these two days at the office were going to totally suck. Aubrey had to use her last couple of days of vacation or else she would lose them come the first of January...so I was stuck at work without my best friend to keep me company and make the mind-numbing boredom more tolerable.

It didn't help matters too much that I was in a bad mood...and to be honest, as bored as I might get - I was conflicted. Just the thought of being apart from Aubrey made my stomach hurt, but then secretly I was sort of glad that I wouldn't see her for a couple of days. I knew I had a lot of thinking to do, but the inconsistency of my thoughts and feelings was maddening. I inwardly knew that my ill temperament centered around the fact that the mental closet in my head was full. I couldn't force any more of these confused feelings and mixed up emotions into it even if I tried.

I took a deep breath and sighed as I set my bag down at my work station. My cell phone vibrated. Aubrey was calling me. Not now, Meg, I told myself. I had been avoiding her calls and not answering her texts since leaving her apartment yesterday morning. It was more than obvious that we needed to talk and avoiding her was just rude...but I didn't know what to say. I needed to sort my sorry self out first. I sighed again.

I docked my laptop, hit the power button and while it went through the process of booting up, I got myself situated for the day. I plugged in my phone charger and then hooked my phone up to charge. After sitting down and getting comfy, I logged in and read my new emails and took the time to respond to a few of them. Alrighty then...there was five minutes of my day. I sighed yet again and settled back in my chair to surf the web for a while. Nope, wasn't working. My mind kept coming back around to Aubrey. My phone vibrated again. It was Aubrey so I let it go to voicemail. I felt like I was at war with myself.

Is she or is she not your best friend? Of course she is. Then why won't you talk to her? I just...need some time to think. Do you care about her? Obviously - thus the whole best friend thing. Do you love her? Again, of course I do. She's the closest friend I've ever had. Okay...but do you love-love her? What? Why would you ask that? I'm not a lesbian. That may be...but you didn't answer the question, did you? Enough...just shut up.

I stood up in frustration from all these questions bouncing around in my head and decided I needed a cup of coffee. I walked across our work area and out of the marketing department section of the second floor. I headed to the little kitchenette / coffee service area that was over near the restrooms. I looked up and saw that Ted from the National Sales team was carefully constructing a large mug of coffee. He was busy adding cream and sugar and some flavor add-in syrup that I never touched. He was wearing a ridiculous looking Santa hat on his head.

I patiently stood behind him and waited my turn.

He glanced over his shoulder, saw me and gave me a big smile. "Morning, Meghan."

"Good morning," I nodded politely.

"How are you, today?"

"I'm good, Ted...and you?"

"I'm just as jolly as can be," he chuckled and licked a couple of his fingers clean from his coffee mess. He moved his big head around on his thick neck as if he were searching for something which made the little snowball on the end of his hat bounce around. "Hey, uh...where's your partner?"

I felt my stomach drop at his use of the word 'partner'. Isn't that what gay couples called each other when they were in a serious relationship or married or whatever?

"Excuse me?"

"Oh, uh, I was just asking about Aubrey," Ted clarified in kind of a sing-song voice. "You know, with you two where there's one there's usually the other."

"What's that supposed to mean?" I snapped and folded my arms across my chest.

"Oh...well, I, uh, just meant that I usually see you two together," Ted immediately turned around with a confused look forming on his face.

"We're not always together," I shot back defensively and I could hear the shrillness creeping into my voice.

"Okay," he nodded slowly and picked up his mug. He started to walk around me in a wide berth and then cautiously asked, "Is, uh, everything okay, Meghan?"

"Yes," I sighed miserably and stepped forward and grabbed a cup. "Everything's fine."

"Oh...okay," Ted kept his distance. Just before he walked off he called out, "Well, uh, Merry Christmas."

"Merry Christmas, Ted," I mumbled almost to myself and dumped out the cup of coffee I had just poured into the sink. I didn't want coffee. I just wanted to go home.

I went back to my desk and sent my boss and the HR manager a quick email claiming that I wasn't feeling well and needed to go home. I didn't care if I got paid or not, I just wanted to go home and crawl under the covers.

****

I hardly even remembered driving home. My body was on autopilot as my mind seemed a jumble of sharp edged emotion and overwhelming turmoil. I parked and went inside. I felt restless. I paced and I ranted to myself as I wandered aimlessly around my apartment trying to think. I also kept avoiding Aubrey's texts and calls. My mind kept coming back to the same question over and over again. What do I want? I couldn't seem to come up with any kind of real answer. I was tired, but didn't sleep, couldn't sleep. I just continued to aimlessly walk around my apartment for a while and then out of frustration I'd sit down and flip through TV channels. I lost all track of time as I continued to marinade in this emotional quagmire.

At some point I looked at the clock and realized it was Tuesday. Really? Already? How did that happen?

It was only 5:30am, but I went ahead and called in sick to work again. I hope I would still have a job come New Year's. I also continued to ignore Aubrey's efforts to try and get hold of me. I was driving myself crazy and at some point later that morning I was so exhausted that I finally fell asleep on the couch. I ended up sleeping for most of the day, but it was a fitful slumber so I woke up still feeling fatigued. I couldn't seem to settle my thoughts. As a result of my exhaustion I finally just zoned out under a blanket and watched old Christmas movies. Even though I'd seen it at least a hundred times, I cried myself silly when I watched It's a Wonderful Life.

I was making myself miserable. I was miserable. Out of frustration I yelled at my empty apartment until I was hoarse and then beat up one of my throw pillows. I was tired of all of the confusion and indecision in my head. Why couldn't this just be simple? I finally just kind of flopped back into a corner of the couch. I ended up watching another old black and white movie. I could not tell you what it was called or what it was about. I honestly don't even remember calling, but somehow I ended up eating Chinese takeout.

I fell asleep on the couch again in that same position. I woke with a start and winced at the crick in my neck. I blinked my eyes around my dark apartment and squinted at the cable box. It was Wednesday morning...Christmas Eve day. I looked at the food containers on my coffee table along with the empty bottle of wine. I was a mess. My mouth tasted like the bottom of a trash can, my hair was a tangled bird's nest. I was still in the wrinkled work outfit from Monday. I smelled horrible and I had stains on my blouse. I needed some help. I got up and headed straight to the shower. After emerging clean and feeling somewhat better, I threw on my comfiest sweats and grabbed my car keys.

I had to talk to the only person I knew would understand.

****

I walked up the front steps of my parent's house and didn't bother knocking. I opened the front door and was met with the heavenly smells of something delicious baking. My mouth watered as I looked around at the empty living room.

"In here, Sug," Auntie Kate called out from the kitchen.

She always called me Sug which was short for "sugar". I was her one and only great-niece and she had always doted on me since the day I was born. I found out that my Mom and Dad were at some volunteer event to serve breakfast at one of the homeless shelters and then afterwards they were going to do some last minute Christmas shopping. Auntie Kate had stayed behind to make some of her world famous goodies for Christmas Eve. She had the whole house smelling of cinnamon and vanilla.

"Sit down," she instructed by pointing a spatula at one of the stool seats at the island.

I did as I was told and as soon as I sat down she put a bowl of what was once icing in front of me. It obviously needed to be cleaned up. I took my finger and ran it down the edge like I used to do when I was little and then sucked the remnants off my finger. My great aunt watched me continue licking the bowl for a moment. I nervously avoided making eye contact. I wasn't sure what to say. I saw her smile out of the corner of my eye and then turn back to whatever deliciousness she had been working on.

"So..." Auntie Kate said without turning around from the counter where she was spooning raspberry preserves into delicate little cups of half-baked pastry dough. "Tell me."

"I, uh..." I started to say and stopped. As soon as I my mouth opened my eyes went all blurry with hot tears. Auntie Kate always knew when something was bothering me and could get to the heart of things quicker than anyone I knew. I started to say something else and then just broke down and began sobbing in earnest.

My Aunt wiped her hands on her apron and took me in her comfortably familiar arms. She put my head on her soft bosom and rocked me gently back and forth and soothed her hand through my hair until I was all cried out. When I finally got control of myself, she fetched me a glass of water for my crying-induced hiccups and then wiped my face clean with a damp cloth. She rested her hand lovingly against my check and smiled warmly at me.

"Feel better?"

"Yes, ma'am," I hiccupped and then felt like I might start crying again. "No...not really."

"Tell me," Auntie Kate said again and then took my face in both of her hands and kissed my forehead. "From the beginning, Sug."

So I did. I mean, I left out some of the details of course (you know, the sex stuff), but I told her everything from my first day at work and meeting Aubrey all the way up to the conversation with Ted at the coffee service Monday morning. I didn't hold anything back. I not only told her the actual stuff, but also how I felt. I mean I just let everything from that mental closet come out...all of it. She simply listened as she put together more pastries, nodding her head as I talked. I knew she was listening closely to every word I said. When I ran out of words, she slid one of her freshly baked treats in front of me and lovingly stroked the top of my head.

"What should I do?"

"Well...I can't rightly say, Sug," Auntie Kate shrugged and just gave me a sympathetic smile. "You're the only one who knows that answer for sure...and you know that."

"Yes, but --"

Kate held up a finger, cutting me off. She walked over to me and gave me another warm hug. It made me feel immediately better. She finally released me and walked over to the kitchen table. She grabbed the humongous bag that served as her purse and opened it up. She gave me another smile as she dug a very old leather bound folder out of the oversized pocketbook. She brought the folder over to the island and carefully pulled a piece of very fancy, expensive looking stationery out of it. She laid the piece of paper gently on the countertop in front of me and then produced a matching envelope from the folder. Lastly, she dug around in the pocket of her apron and then handed me a very expensive looking fountain pen.

"Do you remember this?"

I nodded.

"Have y'all been keeping up with it?"

"Not really," I admitted with a shrug. "I guess it's been a few years."

"Well, now that you're grown, I think you should go on and rekindle it," Auntie Kate decided for me.

She was referring to an old family tradition that we used to do when I was a child. During the week of Christmas each person in the family would write down their deepest wish for the coming year. It was supposed to be that one thing that they didn't think they could live without. Auntie Kate had always insisted that you had to be honest and only write down "that which you most truly desired" was how she had always put it. Then we would put the written wish in an envelope, seal it and leave it in our stockings for Santa on Christmas Eve.

She called it our One True Christmas Wish.

I chewed my bottom lip as I stared into Auntie Kate's twinkling blue eyes. I looked back down at the piece of stationery and slowly picked up the fountain pen.

"Ah-ah-ah," Auntie Kate laid her hand on my arm with a chuckle. "You have to give it some thought, Sug. Remember - it has to be the one thing that you want more than anything else."

****

I went back to my apartment, but not before Auntie Kate had packed me up a little Christmas tin full of her freshly baked goodies. I kissed her on the cheek and promised her I would come back over later that evening. Funny, but I didn't even realize that I had kept one hand on top of that tin for the entire ride back to my place until I pulled into my parking space. I sat in my car for a few moments holding that tin of cookies and pastries and then looked at the stationary and envelope I had set beside it. I gathered up my things and went inside.
I sat down on my couch and rested my arms on my knees with my hands folded in front of me. I stared at my hands for a while.

Okay...enough. This wasn't me. I've never acted like this before in my life, so why the hell was I doing it now? It was time to stop acting like the scared, indecisive little girl that I had been for the past three days and start acting like the capable, independent woman that I truly was. I had finally come to a decision.

I closed my eyes and took a deep breath. I stood up and fetched Auntie Kate's piece of expensive stationary with the matching envelope. I set them down on the couch cushion and then got busy cleaning up the mess I had made out of my coffee table. I quickly washed the few dishes in the sink, tidied up my living room and then sat back down on the couch. I carefully placed that almost mystical piece of paper on the coffee table in front of me. I lined up the envelope right next to it and then dug the fountain pen out of my purse and set it down gently next to the blank stationary. I took a deep breath and let it out slowly.

I knew exactly what I needed to do.

****

Satisfied, I sealed the envelope. I got undressed and decided I was going to take another shower. I took my time washing and conditioning my hair and then scrubbed the fatigue out of my body with my shower sponge thingy. I took my time doing my hair and make-up. I checked the clock on my phone while I curled my hair. I swear it felt like I had been up for hours, but it was only 8:51am. I couldn't wait any longer. I reached over and hit a button on my phone and put it on speaker. I wrapped another piece of hair around the curling iron while I listened to the satellite connect or whatever, but Aubrey must have turned her phone off because it went straight to vm...that or she wasn't taking my calls. I nodded. If that was the case, I understood. I deserved it.

I stood naked in front of my closet. I wanted to dress up. I took my time and chose a very pretty bra and panty set that Aubrey had helped me pick out. I slipped them on and then spritzed myself with some of my favorite perfume - again that Aubrey had helped me pick out. I went through my closet and decided on a nice skirt and sweater outfit. I put on some matching tights and finished it off with a pair of really cute boots. It was really cold outside and I was dressed weather-appropriately, but I also looked damned good, too.

I tried calling Aubrey again...no answer. I sent her a text...no response.

I knew it was my own fault she wasn't responding to me. I just hoped I could make her understand why I had been so distant the last couple of days. I called Aubrey again on my way to her apartment. I also tried her again as I waited in the drive-thru of

Starbucks. I tried Aubrey one last time from her parking lot before I finally decided I would probably have better luck by simply knocking on her door.

I wrapped my knuckles on her door. No answer. I knocked harder. I knew she was home as I caught the faint sound of a slamming door from somewhere inside. I pounded my fist on the door again and waited. I patiently asked her to please answer the door over and over again. I finally ended up pleading and begging. I finally announced that we needed to talk and I wasn't leaving until she opened the door.

I waited and waited outside of her apartment. I paced around a little and stamped my feet to keep warm. I was technically "inside" her building, but the hallway was really more like a tunnel that ran completely through her apartment building from one side to the other. It was maybe ten degrees warmer than the temperature outside. I finally ended up huddling down next to her door and hugging my knees to my chest. I was starting to get really cold by the time Aubrey cracked her apartment door open. I had been sitting outside for at least thirty minutes.

It took me a minute to get my frozen joints to cooperate before I could stand up and face her. She wouldn't look me in the eye, but I could tell she'd been crying. I asked her if I could come in for a minute. She shook her head, but I softly asked her to please just hear me out for a minute and then I would leave if she wanted me to. Without a word she finally stepped aside and held the door open.

Aubrey took the tray of cups from me and set it on the kitchen table. She walked over to the microwave and stuck one of the cups in it. She punched a button and just stood there, silently avoiding eye contact until the microwave finally beeped. She took the cup of coffee out and unceremoniously handed it to me. I was grateful for the warmth on my numb fingers as I followed her into the living room. I watched Aubrey sit down on her couch and I sat across from her in the chair. She still wouldn't meet my gaze.

"Aubrey," I began quietly and had to clear my throat. "I want you to know how truly sorry I am."

She didn't say anything. She just shrugged one of her shoulders and continued not looking at me.

"Aubrey," I pleaded softly. "Please? I just...can you please talk to me?"

She signaled her disapproval with a small grunt and shook her head as if she couldn't believe I had the nerve to ask her that.

"I understand you're upset...you have every right to be," I continued rambling. "If I could just...if you would let me explain --"

"You know what?" Aubrey suddenly spoke up. "I don't care." She shook her head again and said almost as if to herself, "I should've known better."

"Should've known better...how?"

"That it was too good to be true."

"What was?"

Aubrey just shook her head as she stared in the opposite direction.

"What was?" I insisted. "What was too good to be true?"

"You," she said accusingly, "being my friend."

"Aubrey," I replied patiently. "I am your friend and you know it."

"Whatever," she scoffed and crossed her arms across her chest.

"Aubrey," I sighed, but she cut me off.

"You're just like everybody else I've ever trusted, Meghan," she shook her head as she said that and I thought I saw a tear roll down her cheek. I knew she had meant that to sound bitchy, but I thought it sounded sad.

"No, Aubrey," I replied and leaned forward in my seat. "I'm not."

"Really?" she asked incredulously. "Well, gee - you kind of snuck out of here Sunday without so much as a goodbye...and then you just totally blew me off."

"I know," I closed my eyes and dropped my head in shame. "I'm really sorry...I just..."

"Just what?" she snapped and looked in my direction for a brief moment. She looked away again and continued. "I really needed to talk to you...and guess what? You weren't there for me, were you?"

I didn't say anything as I stared at my boots.

"Were you?" she demanded.

I reluctantly shook my head. "No."

"Exactly," she pointed out and was at least looking in my direction if not at me as she chastised me. "You wouldn't take my calls. You didn't answer my texts. So how does that make you different?"

I reached into my purse and pulled out the sealed envelope. I extended my arm towards Aubrey.

"Whatever that is," Aubrey turned her head away from me, "I don't want it."

"Aubrey," I pleaded. "Please take it."

"Forget it," she sighed and slumped back deeper into the cushions of the couch like she was exhausted. "I think you should go."

"Aubrey --"

"Just..." she said more firmly and still wouldn't look at me. "Go."

"Aubs," I whispered still holding the envelope towards her. "Please?"

She just turned her head further away from me and crossed her arms again.

I stood up and slowly walked to the door. I stopped and looked at her. "I wanted to tell you that my family has this tradition --"

"Meghan," she sighed heavily. "I don't care --".

"Let me finish," I raised my voice a little, speaking over her protest firmly. She fell silent and I took that as permission to continue. "See, my Auntie Kate reminded me of it this morning. We had this thing we used to do when I was a kid that she called our One True Christmas Wish. The week of Christmas we were supposed to write down that 'one thing which we most truly desired' was how she always put it. We would seal it in an envelope and on Christmas Eve we were supposed to put it in our stocking."

Aubrey didn't say anything, but at least she was sort of looking in my general direction again as she listened.

"Auntie Kate thought I should get back to that tradition," I explained. "At first I thought it was silly...but then...I don't know, the more I thought about it the more I realized that those envelopes were always gone on Christmas morning. Even when Auntie Kate wasn't with us on Christmas, they somehow disappeared...I guess I never paid all that much attention to it with presents to open and everything."

I took a deep breath before I continued. "And the more I thought about it, the more I realized that when I took a step back... Well, I'm not really sure how to say it, but back when I - I don't know, I guess - believed? Anyways...those years that I did that and I wrote down what in fact was what I wanted most of all way deep down in my heart? It occurred to me that more often than not, in one way or another...my Christmas wishes always ended up coming true."

Aubrey was now finally looking directly at me with this neutral expression on her face. I held the envelope up so I was sure she saw it and then carefully placed it on the little catch-all table next to her door.

"You can open it...you can throw it away...or you can burn it," I instructed her. I grabbed the handle of the door and pulled it open. "But I just wanted you to know that I'm sorry it took me so long to figure things out...but I finally did."

I hesitated a moment longer to try and keep my voice from breaking. "Merry Christmas, Aubs."

With that I turned around and walked out the door without another word, shutting it behind me. By the time I walked down the hall-tunnel to the front entrance of her building I felt like my heart was literally breaking into pieces. I pushed the heavy exit door open and somewhere deep in my brain it registered that it had started snowing again. Some of the big, fat snowflakes were landing on my face and immediately melted on my flushed cheeks and mixed with my tears. I slowly started walking in the general direction of my car, but everything looked blurry as the tears came faster.

"Wait!" I heard Aubrey call out from behind me. "Meg! Wait!"

I turned around to see her running after me. I also saw that she was barefoot and hadn't even bothered to put a jacket on. I immediately took a step towards her in concern. "Are you crazy? You're gonna freeze!"

Aubrey didn't answer as she practically slammed into me, her arms grabbing me in a fierce hug that almost took both of us off of our feet. I saw that she had opened the envelope and had the piece of paper clutched tightly in her fist. We hugged for a long time and then she pulled back and looked into my eyes, tears running down her face too.

"Did you mean it?" she asked breathlessly.

I nodded and we both started crying harder and resumed our hug.

We held each other like we would never let go, but then my common sense finally kicked back in and I shooed her back towards her apartment. She wouldn't take her arms from around me, so the walk was awkward and slow. Her teeth were chattering by the time we got inside. I sat her down on the couch and hurried to her linen closet and grabbed a couple of blankets and wrapped her up in them. She was still clutching that fancy piece of paper in her trembling hand. I looked down at it and read my own handwriting.

My One True Christmas Wish is...Aubrey.

She looked up at me and managed to ask through her chills. "W-why d-didn't you t-tell me?"

"I don't know," I shrugged and looked down at my boots. "To be honest...I really didn't even know how to tell myself."

Aubrey smiled and leaned forward so that her head was resting against my stomach. I put my arms around her shoulders and held her. I shuffled my feet and managed to sit down beside her while continuing to hold her. I kept my hands busy rubbing her back and arms as I tried to help her warm up. She finally stopped shivering and we just kind of sat there leaning against each other with our arms around each other. I pulled away from her a little and took a deep breath. She turned her head and I looked directly into her eyes.

"Look, Aubs...I'm not a lesbian. I'm not attracted to women," I informed her in a quiet, serious voice and I thought I saw a brief flash of confusion in her eyes. For a second I thought she was going to say something, but then she must have thought better of it when she realized I wasn't finished.

"I just know that..." I continued. "That I am attracted to you...very attracted. So if that makes me gay, then I guess I'm gay. I don't care and I honestly don't have it all figured out, but I the one thing that I do know for sure is...I love you."

There...I'd said it. I was not only able to admit it to myself out loud, but I'd confessed it to Aubrey. I found it hard to swallow. My heart was laid bare and it was out there to be accepted...or you know, to be shattered into a million pieces. I held my breath.

"Meg," Aubrey said quietly and those amber-brown eyes looked at me without blinking. She was doing that oh-so-cute little lip-biting thing that I found adorable and was pretty sure she didn't even know she was doing. She shrugged off the blankets and adjusted her position a little so that she was facing me.

Ruh-roh...warning bells of impending doom started going off in my head...Danger, Will Robinson, danger!

"I love you, too."

My heart felt like it had just fallen into the pit of my stomach as I watched the slightest grin pull at the corners of those pouty lips. Wait...what did she just say?

"What?"

Instead of replying she scooted over a few more inches until she was sitting right beside me on the couch. She brought her hands up tentatively and hesitated. We looked into each other's eyes for a few moments. Before I knew what was happening she was gently taking my face in her hands and our heads moved forward like it was in slow motion and then... Then our mouths pressed together and Aubrey's full, pouty lips seemed to fit perfectly against mine. We were sharing our first real kiss.

That kiss was...whew (which you can take the definition of whew to mean WOW...Holy freaking smokes!). I mean, as gorgeous and voluptuous and utterly sensual as everything about Aubrey is, I probably should not have been surprised by our first kiss...but I was. I've never been kissed like that before. Our mouths opened slightly at the same time and Aubrey's felt so delicate and soft. I was completely unprepared by how intimate and passionate it would be to kiss this person who had completely captured my heart. I let out this tiny little sigh as my head started spinning and the whole world just kind of faded away for a few minutes.

We finally broke the kiss and pulled apart. I looked at Aubrey breathlessly.

"I said," she smiled and affectionately kissed the tip of my nose, "that I love you, too."

"Seriously?" I could feel the silly grin spreading across my face. "You do?"

"Uh, it's kind of obvious," Aubrey rolled her eyes and smiled. "That's kind of why I needed to talk to you."

My eyes grew wide and then I jumped and started yelping. She was tickling my ribs as she added with a fake growl, "You know, when you wouldn't return my calls."

"I'm so sorry," I replied and made a sad face, but she stopped me by putting a finger to my lips.

"No more apologies," she insisted. She pulled her finger away, but replaced it with her mouth and we kissed again. She ended the case way too soon in my humble opinion. "I get it...I understand you had to figure this out. I did, too...I guess it just didn't take me as long."

I smiled and felt like maybe I wouldn't be able to stop anytime soon. "I feel like we should...I don't know, go out and celebrate or something."

"Uh-uh...nope," Aubrey shook her head firmly like she had already decided. "We don't have time...Christmas Eve, remember? We have to go to my parents' house and then over to see your family."

"Oh...right," I slumped as that realization hit me. "Soooo...rain check?"

Aubrey stood up. Even though she didn't have any make-up on and her eyes were still a little swollen from crying and her feet and the bottom part of her calves were kinda dirty from running outside barefoot in the snow and her hair was kind of a mess...even with all that, when she looked at me and held her hand out for me to take it? She had never looked more beautiful.

"I have a better idea."

****

Despite the many times we had played around, seen each other naked and had our "fun", I still felt really nervous when Aubrey took my hand and led me down the hall towards her bathroom. I had no idea what was going to happen, but was kind of relieved when she lit a candle and kept the lights off. It gave the entire bathroom a comfortable feel and helped me relax. I stood and watched as she pulled the glass shower door open and turned on the water.

Aubrey turned back towards me with this coy little smile on her face. She stepped closer to me and took hold of the hem of my sweater. My hands were shaking as I lifted my arms and let her pull it up and over my head. I was scared, but a good scared. It was more like overly excited, but at the same time I wanted to do everything right for her. I leaned over and tried to help her out by unzipping my boots, but she playfully slapped my hands away and insisted on taking them off herself. Next, off came my skirt, then my tights until I was standing in front of her in just my bra and panties. Aubrey paused to give me a light kiss on my lips which nearly made me swoon. While she was kissing me she unhooked my bra and gently slid the shoulder straps down my arms.

The bathroom was starting to fill with steam so I wasn't cold, but my nipples were like hard little pebbles. I shivered as her fingers danced along my hip bones and then she slipped those fingers into the sides of the waistband of my panties. I took a shuddering breath as she slowly slid them over my hips and down my thighs, Aubrey going to her knees in front of me as she did so. She was focused on untangling the underwear from around my feet, but once that was done she looked up at me. I watched her face expectantly as I felt her hands slide up along the outside of my thighs. She smiled up at me as her hands traced around to the back of my thighs and then she gently cupped both cheeks of my ass and pulled me closer.

I couldn't help the gasp that escaped my throat when she kissed me on my lower abdomen right above my mons. Her lips felt soft and warm on my skin. Aubrey kissed higher towards my bellybutton as she began to stand up and kissed me again right between my breasts as she fully regained her feet. She let her hands gently caress up my back and then over to run up and down my arms a few times before leaning in and lightly kissing me on the lips again. Then she took a step back and extended her arms towards me.

It was my turn.

I took a deep steadying breath and decided I'd had enough of my jittery nerves. Aubrey was here with me because she wanted to be...and I wanted to be with her. I boldly stepped a little closer and grabbed the bottom edge of her long-sleeved t-shirt. She helpfully put her arms up over her head without being asked and I slipped her shirt up and off. I put my arms around her and ran my nails up and down her naked back which caused her to shudder and I glanced down to watch her nipples harden through the sheer material of her bra. I boldly unhooked it and then pulled it down off of her shoulders. I leaned back and was once again amazed all over again as her large, rounded breasts were revealed to me.

Without asking and without any hesitation I lifted my hands up and ever so softly cupped the heavy orbs in my hands. I lifted them, smiling at the weight and volume of them in my palms. I think I surprised Aubrey as I released them as I expect she thought I'd linger for a while. Instead, my fingertips trailed down her sides and I smoothly hooked them inside the waistband of both her yoga pants and her panties. I followed her lead by sliding them both off over her hips and ass and down her smooth thighs. I lowered myself down to kneel on the floor as I did so.

I focused my attention on getting her clothes clear of her cute little feet. I knew my face was mere inches away from Aubrey's sex. I was holding my breath and as brave as I was trying to be, this was a big moment. I neatly folded Aubrey's yoga pants and then her panties. I knew I was stalling as I set them down on the floor with her shirt and her bra. I kept my eyes down on the floor as I took another deep breath. I raised my head and I was looking directly at Aubrey's pussy. It was just right there in front of my face. I mean I had sort of seen it when we were playing together, but this was different. This was much more intimate.

I leaned a little closer. I hadn't really ever taken the time to look at another woman's vagina before - not from this angle and not this closely. Aubrey's dark pubic hair was very well groomed and for the first time I saw that she shaved her labia and everything below her mons. I couldn't remember what that was called with just the patch of hair above her vagina, but I was fascinated. Aubrey's perfectly proportioned outer lips were slightly parted revealing her almost delicate looking inner lips that were lighter in color. Without asking Aubrey widened her feet a little so that I could just see the glistening hint of her opening. She was already wet. That made me smile. She was wet for me. My eyes trailed up to see that her clit was swollen and starting to peek out from its cute little hood. Just like everything else about Aubrey, I thought her pussy was just beautiful.

I licked my lips and without thinking about what I was doing, I brought my face closer and I guess I just kind of kissed Aubrey right on the pussy. She moaned when I did that. I smiled up at her and stood back up. I slipped my arms around her at the same time that she was reaching for me and we embraced. The warmth of her skin on mine, our breasts pressed together, the heat of our most intimate places pushing closer to each other's was just indescribably erotic to me. I felt...like this was where I was supposed to be...where I belonged.

We kissed again.

With my eyes closed I opened my mouth and felt Aubrey's tongue flicker against my lower lip. I opened my mouth wider inviting her in. Her mouth and tongue were so very soft and it felt like she was massaging the inside of my mouth as she began to tentatively explore. On instinct I reciprocated by softly stroking Aubrey's tongue with my own. Our kiss deepened as our tongues continued to tease and caress and soon her hands were running up and down my back. She cupped both cheeks of my ass and pulled me in tighter. I think I moaned or maybe she did. Either way it made Aubrey smile and then I smiled and we couldn't possibly maintain our kiss.

We pulled apart and she giggled at me as she stepped into the shower. She beckoned me to follow her with a little crook of her finger and that might have been the absolutely sexiest thing I'd ever seen her do. I stepped in under the hot spray of the shower beside her and we couldn't keep our hands off of each other. We touched each other, caressed each other's bodies and mutually explored every inch and curve. We did manage to actually shower and I thought I was in heaven when she washed my hair. I returned the favor and I have to admit that with every switch of position and shift of our bodies her large breasts would sway and bump into mine and for some reason that excited me to no end.

I took my time soaping up Aubrey's body and in that darkened shower I savored the way the soap suds streamed over her curves. I really hoped she was as turned on as I was. I finally grew bold enough that I pushed her against the tiles of the shower wall and I grinned at her as I lowered my face to her chest. I kissed the top of each of her generous breasts and then lowered my head until my mouth found her erect nipple. I heard her gasp as I took it between my lips. I reached up with my hand and cupped her other boob filling my palm with as much of her tit as I could fit in it. I began to massage and squeeze it as I sucked harder on her nipple, tickling it by flicking it with my tongue.

Aubrey brought her hands up to hold my head as I began alternating licking and sucking one nipple and then I moved my head over and did the same to her other nipple. I just could not get over how big and round and perfectly shaped Aubrey's breasts were. Aubrey pulled on my hair a little until I relented and stood back up straight to face her. She brought her hungry mouth to mine and we kissed again, but there was much passion and need in it this time. She caught me a little by surprise when she kind of man-handled me by turning me around so that now I was the one pinned against the wall.

Aubrey kissed her way down my neck and now it was her turn to lavish attention on my breasts. The sensations of her mouth on my sensitive skin made gooseflesh pop up all over my body and my already hard nipples tightened and swelled even further. I bit my lip as I felt her mouth close around my right summit and I could not stifle the moan when she suckled me. My palm slapped against the tile of the shower when she gently bit down, the brief flash of pain turning quickly into an overwhelming sensation of pleasure as her tongue swirled around my nipple in tight little circles.

She continued to lick, suck and nibble on my nipple as her other hand ran up my inner thigh and I spread my legs to give her better access. Aubrey ran her finger up and down my slit a few times and then she easily slipped it inside of me. I was panting as she slowly withdrew her finger and then slid it back in even deeper. She did it again and then again and then as she drove her finger even deeper into my core she moved her thumb up and began using the pad to start massaging my clit.

Aubrey took her mouth off of my breast and straightened up to press her lips against mine. She brought her other hand up to my breast and began to softly pinch and pull on my nipple as she kissed me and continued to fuck my pussy with her finger. The hot spray of the shower beat down on both of us as we passionately kissed. It felt like Aubrey's mouth owned mine as she began pinching my nipple harder and she increased the tempo of her finger-fucking. When she added a second finger inside of me I lost it. I came hard. She even had to hold me up when my knees buckled as my orgasm washed over me.

I sagged against her as she gently kissed my neck. When I finally managed to stand up straight she gave her hair one final rinse and turned off the shower. She reached out to the hook beside the shower stall and grabbed a large fluffy towel. We carefully dried each other off and kept stealing kisses every few seconds like a couple of smitten teenagers. We held hands as we walked towards her bedroom.

For the next few hours Aubrey and I made love. Twice...well, three times if you're keeping score...each. We almost lost track of time, but managed to jump up and get ready so that we wouldn't be late to celebrate the holiday with our families.

****

To say that Christmas was memorable would definitely be an understatement.

Aubrey and I ended up coming out to our families that Christmas Eve. Keep in mind that this was all very new and we hadn't even had time to figure out exactly what 'we' were just yet...but we also weren't shy about letting both of our families know we were together and head over heels in love. Aubrey's family was overjoyed and supportive and celebrated their daughter's happiness. I was overwhelmed by how accepted and loved I felt by her parents and aunts and uncles and cousins.

My parents were a little more on the shocked and "what? are you sure? when did this happen?" side of things. My mom even cried a little bit, but I think once they saw how happy Aubrey and I were together it didn't seem like the end of the world after all. I knew they would be fine...they just needed a little time to process it. Of course, having Auntie Kate's unwavering support helped quite a bit. She was amazing. That ageless beauty of a woman who I admired so much and looked up to could not have been any happier for me.

Best of all, she totally approved of Aubrey...but not just in the sexual preference sense. She could have given a hoot about that...no, Auntie Kate enthusiastically approved of Aubrey as a good person with strong character. Someone she thought was worthy of the love of her favorite great-niece.

Auntie Kate's approval meant the world to me.

Waking up in Aubrey's arms Christmas morning was absolutely the best gift I could have asked for. My eyes slowly blinked open and her beautiful face was right in front of mine with the happiest, most contented smile on it. That smile...oh, my...that smile made my heart flutter and sent the butterflies in my stomach into a gymnastics routine. Yep, that smile confirmed to me that My One True Christmas Wish had truly been granted.

Seeing that I was awake, Aubrey scooted her voluptuous curves a little closer and wrapped her arms around me. I wiggle-wormed my body even closer until we were just this intertwined tangle of female bodies. It felt perfect. After cuddling as close together as physically possible, we just kind of laid there and basked in each other's presence for a while. I knew that life and work and problems would eventually show up, but as long as I knew that at the end of the day I could come back to this...no matter what, everything would be okay.

The sun started to sneak up over the horizon and as it slowly crawled higher in the sky it began lightening up the darkness of the bedroom by slipping through the gaps in the blinds. It was

Christmas morning. Aubrey picked her head up and looked into my eyes for a moment. She leaned her face a little closer to mine and gave me the softest, sweetest kiss in the history of kisses. She pulled back and rested her head back down on the pillow. Her smile grew even bigger.

"Merry Christmas," she whispered.

"Yes," I whispered back with a smile. "Indeed it is, my love. Indeed it is."

Explicit Erotic Sex Stories

PLEASE LOVE ME

Catherine harbors romantic thoughts for Vanessa. Will they come together? (Lesbian)

Pamela Vance

Spring of 2011

Catherine

A small number of people were watching the game. It came during all of the women's junior volleyball matches. Normally, you couldn't accommodate a piece of paper amongst the crammed fans while the boys were performing. Catherine didn't notice the absence of a crowd; she wasn't much of a people person in the first place. Her gaze lingered on one individual in particular as she sat there in relative solitude; it was the settler of her school's squad.

Catherine had more than one excuse to be attracted to her; Vanessa was also her closest friend and her greatest crush. It's not the simplest of varieties. Catherine had realized she liked girls when she was fourteen; Vanessa was as clear as an arrow, famous and attractive, with girl-next-door features mixed with the toned firmness that comes from participating in sports from a young age. She has the most beautiful and deep blue eyes you might ever imagine. Her white complexion has a pinkish tinge to it and just a few freckles. Her hair was a shoulder-length golden mane that framed her features beautifully. Catherine found herself daydreaming once more...her body was worth killing over. Catherine squirmed in her seat, just dreaming of her. "Stop!" she admonished herself softly.

Catherine, on the other hand, had finally learned to cope with her crush. It may be painful at times, but she had perfected resilience and stamina by this stage. The sensible part of her mind never stopped reminding her that pursuing straight girls was the road to the Dark Side. Going for a straight girl who happens to be your best friend was a very humiliating pitfall that Catherine was well aware of. But that was the sensible portion of her mind talking; her heart was telling her differently. Although she couldn't simply take her heart out and rebuild it, she did the next best thing: she buried her emotions, wishing and believing that they would go out.

The whistle of the referee and the cheers of the girls jolted her out of her reverie. Alba College had secured just another game and was on the way to the provincial championships. Catherine saw the girls huddled in the middle of the court, cheering and high-fiving each other. After their festivities were done, they made their way to the locker room for a well-deserved shower and change of clothing.

Catherine, as was her habit, proceeded to the locker's exit to await her mate. She was fiddling with her phone absentmindedly until she noticed a pair of hands close her vision.

"Can you guess who?"

"Hmmmm...yes...let me think...warm hands...finger tape already clinging to the fingers of my left hand...hmmmm...and if I do this..."

Catherine reached out her hands and mercilessly tickled Vanessa's bare flanks, prompting her to collapse against the wall in laughter.

"Well, well, well, well, well, well, well, well, well, well Ladies and gentlemen, if it isn't Alba College volleyball sensation, Vanessa Duval!"

Vanessa smirked and put out her tongue.

"That's no tongue sticking, kid, as I've told you a thousand times. You should be able to do this if you stick out your tongue." Catherine slithered her tongue out and smoothly kissed the tip of her nose.

"That's what I wish I could do...

In reality, I'm sure you could lick your boobs with that tongue..."

"What makes you think I'd like to do that, you weirdo?"

"If Nicholas noticed me doing that, he'd cream his socks."

Oh, the ever-present Nicholas, still there to remind Catherine of her friend's honesty.

"Yes, I'm sure you'd be a hit," Catherine admitted rather dejectedly.

"You don't care about him."

"He's all right. If you're pleased with him, I'm pleased with him."

"But you don't want him."

"It's none of my concern. May we please move out of here?"

"What's the matter with you? In any case, let's go... I'm starving... If you want to be a burgher or something?"

Vanessa was a volleyball player, but she took her junk food seriously, particularly after a game. Catherine was still astounded at how much food her friend might eat when remaining in peak condition. If she binged very mildly, she would instantly suffer for it by feeling her denim stretch at the seams.

Catherine listened with interest as her companion devoured her double-cheeseburger. They were sipping their sodas in silence, which was unusual for them until Vanessa wanted to crack it.

"Catherine...I have everything to tell you..."

"Oh no!" Catherine was quickly placed on alert by Vanessa's solemn tone.

"There is no convenient way to put it...

My parents demanded that I apply for scholarships in the United Kingdom. My parents believe that this is for the better..."

"I...uh...but what about your preparations to join Western?"

"They said an international experience would be beneficial..."

"And...and...how are you, what are your thoughts?"

"I," you say.

"How are our arrangements to attend the same university?"

In silence, Vanessa stooped her forehead. Catherine had the sensation that she had been struck by a moving train. Catherine and Vanessa, Catherine and Vanessa... They're as similar as two peas in a pod. Best mates will be best friends for the rest of their lives. Catherine was the silent thinker, while Vanessa was still the guiding power. Catherine was the bookworm, while Vanessa was the runner. Yet they were so well matched that they could feel each other's emotions without ever speaking to each other.

And now Catherine felt as though a piece of herself was being ripped away. She blinked her eyes shut, hoping to halt the flood of tears that she sensed was on its way, but it was futile. Rivulets began to shape, and her vision became fuzzy.

"Can we please go outside? I...I need some fresh air."

Fighting back her emotions, Catherine stood up and dashed out the entrance, Vanessa close behind.

"Hello, Catherine! Wait a minute! Wait a minute!"

Catherine leaned on a nearby table, brushing her eyes away with the palm of her hand. She raised her bloodshot eyes to Vanessa.

"I'm sorry, Catherine..."

"No...hey...I'm the one who has to apologize...

I'm a complete wimp. It's just that you dropped quite the bombshell on me. I...um...um...um...um...um...um...um...um...um You'll do doing right... I'm certain you'll shine everywhere you go."

"I'm not abandoning you, Catherine. It isn't... For Christ's sake, I'm not going to the moon! We'll speak! We'll talk on Skype! You are welcome to come over anytime you want! Come on, let's go! Please, pleeeeeeeeeeeeeeeeeeeeeeeeeeeeeeeeeeee"

Catherine sent her a waning grin. They had made too many arrangements together, all the way down to the most minor level. They'd already found a place to live off-campus. But Vanessa, ever the motivator, had modified the plans. Catherine was used to many improvements, but this was a real kick in the gut. Maybe it was for the better, she reasoned. Through her strongest attempts to hide her best mate's feelings, Catherine secretly fantasized about seducing her straight best friend. Fate had made a different decision. She put on a fake grin.

"Princess Leia would suffice. As your highness directs."

"Anakin, Anakin! I've always advised you not to bend in front of me in public. It warns the paparazzi, and they come for me like TIE soldiers."

"Yes, your most illustrious highness. I swear I'll be nice."

It was the end of it. Vanessa had charted her path, as she often did, and Catherine had agreed. Catherine reasoned more and found that it was safer this way. Since she was not as accessible as her friend perceived her to be, her sexual orientation existed a tightly buried mystery inside her. What she'd do about it was a different matter.

Vanessa

It had gone better than she had expected, Vanessa reflected once she was back in her bed. As she affectionately referred to her, she was certain Anakin was hiding something from her, but she didn't want to put too much pressure on her at the moment. There was no need to press her luck anymore after she'd gotten away from the bomb she'd dropped on her.

She continued with her beauty regimen, content with herself. Vanessa was not a poor individual by any means. It's just that she enjoyed being the object of attention now and again. It's not that she did consciously; it's just that becoming an only child brought this action to the surface at times.

Vanessa was stunning in every way. As much she could tell from the boys' whistles and cat-calls. Other than the boys' stares, the girls' eyes revealed their envy and jealousy. She, on the other hand, was not for bullying and drawing unwelcome publicity. She wore comfortable clothes to school and was often seen in athletic wear. She spent more time at the theater with her friends, especially Catherine, watching the latest sci-fi blockbuster. Vanessa, like Anakin, was a Star Wars fanatic. She'd also suited up as a stormtrooper once, complete with headgear. She had decided to dress up as Princess Leia, Jabba the Hutt's slave, but her mother had nearly died of frustration. Speaking of rage, she still needed to keep up with her Taurine Warrior soon, now that the zillionth WoW update had arrived.

"Oh my God! I'm going to have to scramble here! If I stand him up AGAIN, Nicholas will be furious, "She pondered. She added the final touches to her make-up and tested herself in the mirror in a whirlwind of activity. They were going to the cinema with Nicholas today, and she was especially looking forward to it.

He came to a halt in their driveway just as Vanessa dashed down the stairs.

"And why are you in such a hurry?"

"I'm going on a date with Nicholas, dad."

"Oh, well...

Please be cautious on the highways...

You're also expected to be back by midnight!"

"Yes, dad, bye!"

Catherine

About the fact that it was a Friday night, Catherine was bundled comfortably in her sweatpants and sat in front of her computer display. She was attempting to complete an article on the effect of the Seven Years' War on Canada, but she was having trouble focusing. Her thoughts keep wandering to Vanessa, distracting her from all fruitful jobs. "Perhaps I need a rest," she reasoned to herself. She squeezed her eyes and rubbed her temples while she removed her glasses.
"Wow, that feels good...maybe I've been working on this for a longer time than I figured." She could sense her abdominal muscles tightening and relaxing as she arched her back in her chair. Her right hand descended from her head and settled on her crotch, offering it a decent grub as her eyes were closed. "Mmmmmmm...that was much better than healthy." Catherine

was a balanced young adolescent who never passed up a decent chance to masturbate while she felt like it. And this gloomy day demanded a release of some kind.

Keeping her eyes closed, she managed to greedily grope her groin with her right hand while cupping her breasts with her hands. Her sweatshirt's cotton lining felt luxuriously electrifying against her breasts, and she soon felt the distinct feeling of moisture permeating her vagina.

Flashes of Vanessa in her volleyball spandex shorts weaved their way across her synapses. Guilty joy fired through her body as her mind ignited visions of her closest friend. Her lips were red, and her clitoris was pressing against the cotton lining of her bra. She could sense the itch as her cunt pleaded to be fondled as she squeezed her thighs closely together. Her wandering hand, dissatisfied with her thighs' constraints, wanted to explore improved access to her throbbing cunt.

Sucking her wind, she moved her fingertips south of her waistband and past the brim of her pantyhose. Grazing her fingertips into her pubic hair just increased her arousal. Her body desperately needed this relief, she reasoned. When her finger made contact with the shaft of her clitoris, she felt every inch of her skin burst out in goosebumps. She rubbed herself with an increasingly growing tempo, her fingertips sandwiched between her thighs.

"Oh my goodness...Oh yeah..."

And her phone rang, the shrill chirping ruining the moment.

"Oh, for God's sake, Vanessa! I'm not fucking fuckingfuckingfucking"

She briskly pulled her hand from her vagina, cursing under her breath and readjusting her sweatpants in the process. She picked up the handset grumpily.

"Of course!"

"I'm sorry...Catherine? Is it you, sir?"

"It's me, Leia," I say.

"Oh...I hope I'm not bothering you in some way..."

"No, I'm good...I was really in the midst of something, but it's fine..."

"You filthy mutt! Who's been sneaking around in your room? Do I recognize him?"

"No one has crept into my bed, Vanessa! I was also waiting to conclude my essay for the Seven Years' War!"

"Oh, well...

Then you're not interested in knowing about my date with Nicholas, are you?"

"Goodbye, Vanessa."

"Oh my goodness...

It was amicable...

We went to the movies together, and I was wearing my short caramel skirt...you know...the one that shows off my butt so nicely and..."

"What exactly is this, a hotline? I think I said I didn't want to know!"

"Are you upset over what happened earlier?"

"What are you talking about? No, it does not... Listen up, Vanessa...No... It's just because you happened to catch me in a bad mood... I've been a first-rate babe today, haven't I?"

"It's cool, Anakin...everyone has bad days...no deep feelings?"

"There are no hard feelings, Leia...

Listen, I'm certain that a decent night's sleep would be beneficial to me. I promise to behave much better tomorrow. How could you come over in the morning and tell me everything?"

"You've got a good one, sister! I'll be by your house around...tennish?"

"Yes, indeed. And I'll see you later..."

Catherine turned off her cell and threw it to the side of her bunk. "Vanessa, you're a jerk! Good luck with the awards for poor timing, kid." She reasoned that it was equally her responsibility. She should have dismissed it or set it to silence. She attempted but failed to complete what she had begun. Excellent! She was now faced with dirty underwear and an agitated cunt. Only what she wanted to put an end to this dreadful day.

Vanessa

Vanessa waited at the front door of the Blickman residence. Catherine's mother arrived at the front entrance.

"Good morning, Mrs. B. Is Catherine here?"

"Good morning, Vanessa. Please come in. Yes, she is operational. Would you like to join us for breakfast or go straight to her room?"

"Thank you, Mrs. B. I'm fine. For the time being, I'll just go upstairs."

"I'll see you two later."

Vanessa hopped up the stairs into Catherine's apartment, following a route she must have followed thousands of times before. "I think I won't be seeing this staircase soon," Vanessa reflected, a pang of regret in her heart. She barged through Catherine's bedroom entrance, only to discover an almost naked woman. Catherine stood in front of her mirror, dressed only in her pantyhose, her hair soaking wet. Catherine almost flew to the ceiling, instinctively covering her breasts with her palms.

"Oh, Lord, you scared the hell out of me! Don't you have any doors at your house? You remember, knock-knock and all that?"

"I'm sorry...

I guess I was forgetful. By the way, you look adorable in those."

"I mean? Still, what are these stretch marks?"

"What nonsense are you on to, girl? You're wonderful! We all have them; I have them, and you do as well. There is nothing to feel embarrassed about. We're regular ladies, not toothpick Photoshop models!"

"But you're so lean and thin, and your girls are so proud of you! Look at my pathetic excuses!"

"And you're taller and have darker skin than me, who is boringly white. You have fantastic curves and a slender waist. You have no freckles! You will spend all day in the sun without fear of turning into a pomegranate. Each time you take a shower, your hair remains straight and doesn't appear as a bomb has landed on your head. You are stunning, Catherine, and don't let anybody convince you differently."

"You're just kind, but thank you nonetheless. Highly admired and desperately required."

Vanessa then began to recount the events of the previous night as Catherine started to dress.

"...and after the movie was done, he brought me to his house. His parents and brother were also off for the night. So we went to his bed, he placed some soft whatever on the floor to play with, and we kissed..."

"yaaaaaaaaaaaaaaaaaaaaaaaaa

"Stop talking, Catherine! You're just jealous...anyway, I offered him a hand-job when he fingered me. He sure messed it up this time! You should have witnessed it!"

"Your explanation has already made me soaking wet. I'll skip on the main course, please!"

"You may be as pessimistic as you like, but it was hot yesterday! Before I go, I hope I'll go the full nine yards with him."

"Did you complete?"

"No, but it felt great, and I had this warm glow after."

"Did he want to kill you after you killed him, or did he just lay there like a suck of spuds?"

"He...you wonder how you can be such a b*tch at times? No, I left soon after that because he said his parents and brother were on their way home."

"Did you later take control of yourself?"

"No way! Why will I do such a thing? That's revolting!"

"It's named m-a-s-t-u-r-b-a-t-i-o-n, and it's a happy feeling. You can give it a shot."

"But I have a boyfriend; why would I do anything like that?"

"But I have a lover...

Princess Leia, you've always got boyfriends...

How many orgasms did they provide you with?"

Vanessa could sense her cheeks turning a rich shade of red as they heated up.

"I...I'm not familiar with Anakin..."

Catherine's posture instantly softened when Vanessa bowed her head in embarrassment.

"Hello, Vanessa...

I apologize...

I didn't mean to bother you...

I apologize. I may be a little snobbish at times. I didn't want to..."

"It's all right, Catherine...

It was all my responsibility...

I just threw my shit on you because you didn't want to hear it...

I was just so pleased yesterday that I decided to share it with you."

"I sincerely apologize, Vanessa...

I...I was acting like a jerk...

You have every reason to be pleased with Nicholas. He's a nice man, and I hope you two have a successful relationship. You did not warrant my wrath, and I apologize."

"Anakin, please acknowledge my apologies...

Now, how about we go shopping before the Saturday stampede?"

"I can't say no, can I?"

"No way."

"So, let's get this done with. Lead the way, your royal highness..."

Summer of 2011

Catherine
"Ah yes...now this is reality," Catherine reflected as she lounged on her towel on the sandy shore. She was wearing headphones, and her iPod was blasting colorful songs through her face.

"What are you listening to, this goddamn retro shit?"

"What are you talking about? I can't understand you until you speak louder!"

"I SAID...forget about it!"

Vanessa pulled one of her best friend's ear plugs out and inserted it into her own.

"What exactly are they? They sound...foreign?"

"I touch myself, Divinyls. Take note of these facts!"

"Yes, I see...

Is there any possibility you'll follow the rest of us?"

"It depends on whom I'm going to enter."

"Steven came in with a refrigerator full of beer."

"Good luck with your sobriety."

Catherine closed her eyes and removed the ear plug in her ear. This was a tragic error because she didn't recognize Vanessa and a swarm of girls and boys approaching her motionless silhouette.

"Okay, boys...

We grab the legs while you hold the head and weapons. The lake water could jolt her up."

"What the hell...

heyyyyyyyyyyyyyyyyyyyyyyyyyyyyyyyy

No, you cretins...NOOOOO...wait, wait...my iPod...grab my iPod, it can't get wet...VANESSA, YOU BITCH!! No, no, no...come on...it tickles..."

Catherine was thrown into Lake Erie with a loud, abrupt splash. The cold water caused goosebumps on every inch of her face, and her nipples protruded like pencil erasers through the cloth of her bikini.

"Catherine, you look...wet! Oh, then what is that? Are you freezing, or are you relieved to see me?"
Among her colleagues, raucous laughter erupted. "Oh, yeah...laugh it up, people," Catherine said mockingly, although she was grinning. She didn't want to go on this camping trip, but

Vanessa insisted, and in the end, it wasn't such a terrible deal. If she'd ever considered wanting to set her up with men... Yet Catherine suspected her closest friend had good intentions. She was the one who felt bad for keeping secrets from her, but there was no chance she was telling Vanessa about her sexual identity, let alone her hidden crush. If she's guilty or not, she'd rather die with this secret than reveal it to Vanessa.

When the sun began to sink, Catherine made her way to her tent to shift into some colder clothing for the night. She placed on her favorite racerback bra and three-quarter leggings, with a sleeveless shirt on top. She took her windbreaker as she made her way to catch up with the others. They normally started the day with a barbecue and then went to the beach. Catherine hated the moment when she usually had to respectfully refuse an invitation for "a stroll on the sand" or somewhere else the guys decided to drive her. She honestly felt terrible about it because she was familiar with most of them; they had been to high school together, and the guys in their inner group of mates were all good guys. She didn't hate men; she just didn't want to have sexual relations with them.

Night fell, and the sky was quickly full of silvery stars. As the barbeque began to wind down, Catherine became nervous as she saw impromptu couples pairing up. She glanced about nervously; there was this person, Olivia, whom she didn't know very well, a friend of a friend or something. She was wearing earplugs, fiddling with her phone, and seemed to be very bored. "Ah...perhaps my way out for tonight," Catherine reasoned. She approached her, grabbing a bottle of something from the fridge.

"Isn't it Olivia?"

"Sorry...let me remove these...oh, hello there. That's it; it's me!"

Catherine began speaking quickly like she always did when she was anxious. "I apologize for interrupting you in this manner, but I need a favor. My best friend Vanessa has made it her life's mission to match me with one of the boys, and I'm not interested. Will you want to go on a stroll with me?"

Olivia let out a hearty chuckle.

"Oh, yeah, I know...I'm desperate...but caution is the better part of valor."

"No...no...just it's that you standing there with a bottle of wine and asking me for a stroll sounds like such a man thing...it reminds me of...gimme a sec..."

Olivia let Catherine borrow her headphones. She began singing loudly in response to the music they heard: "Hello, I'm new here... And this is insane... So here's my phone number... So give me a call... And the rest of the boys... Try to catch up with me... So here's my phone number... So give me a message..." However, she was unable to finish the album and bent over with laughter. Her chuckle was contagious, and Catherine quickly found herself smiling as well.

"So, putting dumb excuses aside, would you like to go for a stroll with me? I'm in desperate need of new air."

"Sure thing! Only give me a second to get my blanket, and we'll be on our way."

Catherine was perplexed and considered inquiring about the scarf, but she kept her tongue. Maybe she was chilly and didn't have any heavier clothing with her. Olivia quickly followed her, her grin already on her lips. She looked very attractive now that she had caught her attention. She was about a half-foot shorter than Catherine and of medium height. She had a lovely oval face that was outlined by her red hair. She had whitish skin and no freckles and a bright pink flush to her cheeks. Her figure was petite, but the visible bulge of her sweater pointed at huge breasts.

The night was breathtaking; a moonless sky meant thousands of stars strewn through its dim veil, illuminating it with their silvery glow. The sky was so blue that you could see the Milky

Way and all its glory. A warm breeze from the lake was sweeping inland, rendering it comfortable to hang out in only a t-shirt. Olivia chose a comfortable flat area for her blanket, and they stood there, looking at the stars and passing the bottle back and forth.

"Are you Catherine?"

"Yeah, yeah, yeah, yeah, yeah, yeah, yeah, yeah

"I'm drowsy, but the night has been so fun...

I'm not ready to return to my tent just yet. May I lay my head on your lap for a few moments?"

"Uh, sure...sure...go ahead."

Olivia nestled her head in Catherine's lap as she leaned cross-legged. She quickly closed her eyes and leaned her cheek against Catherine's calf. "Well, I think it's a good thing I shaved this morning," Catherine reasoned, adding, "but she's cute..." She began caressing her hair with her hand absentmindedly, to which Olivia replied with a slight purring tone. She immediately removed her hand, alarmed, only to have Olivia replace it on her head.

"Just don't stop...that was fun and soothing."

Catherine's ministrations persisted, encouraged. Her hand soon settled into a rhythm in which it would begin at her temple and eventually make its way in an arc towards her ear. It would stay there, playing with her delicate ridges and sensitive earlobe. It would graze her velvety neck gently until it reached the junction of her collarbone. Her hand will climb once more, cresting her chest, coasting her lips, and thereby finishing the cycle, not daring to step south of that line.

Olivia's eyes were closed, and an angelic grin appeared on her lips. This was the most erotic experience Catherine has ever had. She gazed lovingly at Olivia, wishing the night would never stop. She heard her say, almost in hushed tones:

"Are you Catherine?"

"Are you sure?"

"My back feels a little achy. Will you mind sending those enchanted hands of yours over there?"

"Yeah, yeah, yeah, yeah, yeah, yeah, yeah, yeah, yeah, yeah, yeah, yeah, yeah

Sure thing! Take my windbreaker and use it as a cushion here. It would be more comfortable for you that way."

Catherine couldn't believe her good fortune. She'd fantasized of a moment like this ever since she realized she was physically drawn to other females, with the topic of her reveries almost entirely centered on Vanessa. And now she was alone on the beach with a pretty girl on a sunny summer night.

"Is it you, Olivia? If you might unclasp your bra for me, that will make it simpler for me to rub your back...if you're really up for it..."

Instead of responding, Olivia hid her hands behind her back and underneath her jumper, exposing a sliver of lovely white skin for Catherine to appreciate. Olivia utterly surprised her by extracting the garment from the inside when she wanted her to cut the bra straps from her back merely.

"There...that does no longer concern us..."

Catherine began to glide her palms up and down Olivia's spine, her hands slightly shaking. She couldn't get to all of her back because she was hunched on her feet, and her stance wasn't the most relaxed on the planet. Olivia's previous signals encouraged her to straddle her hips, effectively leaning her groin on the other girl's ass. She kept her breath as she shifted her weight from one leg to the other, expecting some sort of condemnation, but none came.

Catherine continued to knead her back, seeing her silence as acquiescence softly. Olivia's cheek was propped up on her scrunched windbreaker, and her hair was strewn around her makeshift pillow. Her eyes were closed, and her lips were pressed together in a silent grin. A contented sigh would sometimes emerge from inside, indicating that she loved the medication. Catherine, becoming more confident, moved her hands down her flanks, softly pressing on her breasts' spherical bases. Olivia's reaction was to squirm somewhat and thrust her rear upwards into Catherine's groin.

Catherine felt incredibly hot under the neck all of a sudden. Olivia's hands were all over her back, and her slight rubbing on her back had caused normal engorgement in her loins. She was having the most sexual moment of her life, completely unwelcome and out of nowhere. It looked phenomenally sublime to be able to softly rub and grip Olivia's enormous boobs right through her hoodie.

Catherine became more daring, even though her pulse was pounding like a jackhammer, and her mind had long since shut down. She moved her weight lower on Olivia's legs, eventually shifting her focus to her legging-covered thighs and buttocks. The errant movement of her hands became increasingly concentrated on the globular magnificence of Olivia's rear end. Slowly, she would trace her hands across those lovely mounds, beginning at her lower back and working her way to the outsides of her thighs. She'd linger there for a while before her palms, almost with a mind of their own, traversed her biceps and penetrated the amazingly sexy space behind her inner thighs.

Catherine could sense the fire in her hands now; she was shaking, and that had nothing to do with the night chill. She wasn't shivering on her own; Olivia was squirming now, and her legs had spread up slightly.

"Are you Catherine?"

"Y...yeah, yes, yes, yes, yes, yes, yes, yes,

"I...I'd like you to do the front now if that's okay..."

Olivia rotated her body and leaned straight, causing Catherine to pull to the left. Olivia's expression was flushed with glee as her brown eyes locked on Catherine. When they inevitably gravitated towards each other, the gulf between them began to close. Catherine's eyes widened as she reflected on Olivia's slightly parted mouth. Their noses slid together, and their eyes shut. When their lips met, sparks flew. Catherine noticed a burning sensation on hers; it was the most heartwarming sensation she had ever had in her life. That was her first embrace.

They gradually separated. Catherine took her hand up to her mouth unconsciously. Her pulse may be felt on them. Her whole life seemed to be in a deeper level of awareness. Olivia smiled like a thousand watts, and Catherine saw her insides melt like sugar. Their brows furrowed once more; this time, there was no looking back. Their embraces became more intimate and more profound. Olivia cupped one of her cheeks with one palm and leaned the other on the back of her neck. Catherine clung to her, hugging the brunette's lower back.

They began to undress without breaking their kiss, without ever worrying about it. Windbreakers, sweaters, and t-shirts were removed, so both girls were naked from the waist up. Hands now had acres of delicious nude skin to touch, and new, explosive sensations flooded their bodies. Olivia split their kiss and lowered her head towards Catherine's breasts, a mischievous grin on her lips. Catherine drew in her air, anticipating what was about to happen. Olivia let out a light sigh as her tongue made contact with an erect nipple.

Catherine let go of Olivia's waist and arched her spine in a catlike motion. Her hair flailed wildly as she plunged her breast against Olivia's divine mouth. She felt like a dam on the verge of bursting, and all her fairy tale lover had done was suckle on one breast. She thought to herself, "God, this feels amazing." Catherine began to see stars in her vision when Olivia turned her focus to her other breast. Her pants were certainly wet, and she could sense some of the moisture escaping into her leggings.

Just as she figured her happiness couldn't get any bigger, she sensed Olivia's hand snaking down her stomach. Her pelvis launched itself into the air to face the intruder. She was going to climax while completely dressed, she reasoned. Olivia expertly found her clitoris under her leggings and pantyhose and began running her fingertips around it.

Catherine's breathing became more rapid. Her legs were tense, and her muscles bulged and stretched. A warm rumble began in the pit of her stomach and spread across her body like wildfire. Her eyes closed, and her heart stuck in her throat as great, fantastic contractions raced through her body. Her pelvis thrashed as spasm after spasm engulfed her whole being and transported it to incredible new heights of ecstasy. Olivia resumed her ministrations in a much lighter manner, removing the remaining ounces of gratification from her flesh.

"Please...no more... you're too responsive..."

Olivia let go of Catherine's hand and coaxed her to lay next to her on their temporary pillow. Wonderful emotions were coursing through her body as potent endorphins encircled it. She sighed happily, satisfied.

"Wow, that was fantastic...thank you!"

"You're welcome," Olivia said, nodding.

"Are you...uh...you mean..."

"Is she a lesbian? No, I'd call myself a sexual dabbler. Is that what it means to be bisexual? Perhaps... So who cares?"

"Should you...have you ever...I mean...would you think about dating me?"

Olivia burst out laughing. "Would I consider dating you? If I could, Catherine, I will. In August, I'll be heading for Victoria, British Columbia. You listed going to Western Ontario to research. So...I'm not sure...a long-distance fling? It's not exactly my thing...but that doesn't mean we can't have fun before then. You're a stunning and enticing young lady. I'd like to see you again...in truth, I'd like to see you right now..." Olivia punctuated her expression with dart-like kisses to Catherine's ear, saying, "...I think...we...have...some unfinished business remaining!"

They kissed again, but some of the magic had faded for Catherine. They wound up in Olivia's tent later that night. Considering the phenomenal orgasms that the more seasoned Olivia elicited from her body, Catherine was confused as she collapsed in her tent in the early hours of the morning. It was her first experience with another child; she'd taken a massive trip on the pleasure train, and yet...why did she feel that something was missing? She'd give in to her impulses two more times that summer, and each time she'd wind up in Olivia's tent, so that was it. Olivia, true to her expression, vanished late that summer, leaving no trace.

Autumn of 2011

Vanessa

Outside, the sky was an awful dark grey; a slow drizzle was dropping and had been for a few days. Vanessa sat in front of her desktop, which was perched atop her Spartan desk in her similarly sparse flat bed. Her room...a morgue gurney in a freezer actually had more space than this, she reasoned. Come to think about it; there's perhaps more comfort as well. There was a bed with three wide drawers underneath, which meant she had to sleep with her back to the wall every night for fear of slipping off in the middle of the night. And there was a wooden wardrobe and a pair of worn book shelves, and that was it. Oh, but you had paper-thin windows because you could hear if the girl on the first floor were wearing shoes that night or whether her next-door neighbors were fighting like jackrabbits.

For the last two months, her line of thinking has been directed toward her lack of sex. Who only served to irritate her more. She felt somewhat bloated; she'd been PMSing for a couple of days, and when her damned cycle showed up, that might mean hell on earth for the first few hours. She was homesick and confused by her current path and surroundings; she desired a huge embrace and a bowl of ice cream. Speaking of giant embraces, she had to contend with Nicholas acting like a crybaby; his constant online envy was making her nuts, and she was on the verge of firing him.

Above everything, she missed her best friend; she yearned for Catherine's business. Anakin...how could she have imagined that studying abroad would be a smart idea? Catherine had become more melancholy and closed to herself after that fateful decision was announced, but particularly after that summer camping trip. Vanessa was sure that her best friend kept something from her, but she didn't know what it was.

Unable to focus on her idea any longer, she opted to update her Skype; she could use a smiling face right now. Real, Catherine's avatar, Anakin Skywalker, had a bright green tick under it, indicating that she was online. Vanessa wanted to call her; what time was it over there? They had to be four hours late, didn't they? Then it should be well. She noticed the familiar buzzing sound Skype created when it attempted to connect. "Come on...come on...pick up...pick up...please pick up..."

As the link was made, the picture of Catherine appeared on her laptop screen. As Catherine bent over rummaging through her book bag, she could see the familiar surroundings of her BFF's home.

"Wait a minute...I need to retrieve...this perplexed...cell phone from my pocket...

Oh, hello...Vanessa? You appear to be a jerk! What transpired?"

"Don't I seem to be? I'm about to get my time, so..."

"Is that it, or did you have another squabble with...you know who?"

Vanessa snorted and raised her voice in volume. "You'll never hear his name before. What is it about him that you despise too much?"

"I'm not sure...why do you like him?"

"What is that going to mean? For crying out loud, he's my fiance!"

"Okay...all right...

Let us take a step back and take a deep breath here. What exactly did you call me for?"

Vanessa, who was still tired, could sense tears welling up in her eyes. "Maybe this wasn't such a smart plan... I'll contact you again later..."

Catherine instantly detected Vanessa's sadness in her expression, as well as her drooping head. "No way, don't go... Leia's, I apologize... I used to be rude, and you were right to scream at me... Let's start from scratch... If you want to speak to me now, or do you want to contact me later?"

Vanessa buried her head in her arms, sobbing uncontrollably. "I'm so goddamn unhappy... I'm not sure where to go..."

In pain, Catherine almost whispered back, "...no...please don't cry...please Leia..."

Vanessa fished for a Kleenex and managed to gather up her bits after a few minutes of letting the floodgates burst. "Oh my goodness...I'm so sorry... I'm not sure what got into me... That was just what I wanted." "Damned time..." she managed a half-smile.

"Have you had a rough week?"

"Oh my God...where do I begin...

Mr. You-Know-Who, as you said, is being a jerk. He's acting like a stalker on the internet. His enviousness is out of control, and it's making me nuts. If we were back together, I might have abandoned him like he was yesterday's news, but I can't take the long-distance abuse. When I return home for Christmas, he'll be shot... I honestly can't do this long-distance nonsense."

"I know it's not what you want to learn right now, but...I did tell you so. Simply put, the man reeks of insecurity. You don't earn it, Leia... So...what else is there? Let it all hang out...come on...spill...get it out of your mind."

"My Lord...Umm...well...the software here is proving to be much more complex than I expected, as I've previously mentioned.

Sunderland, I suppose, has the same beauty as Cleveland... Oh, but they have great tap beer in both of their bars..."

"Is it you, Vanessa? What else is there?"

Vanessa shuddered, struggling in vain to hold back a cry. "I miss you, stupid... God, I miss you so much it hurts at times...and it's all my fault!"

Catherine's stomach twisted into knots, and she practically put her hands on her core in agony. "You don't play reasonably, Leia," she observed. "...I miss you as well...more than you realize..."

The final words were scarcely audible, but they sounded like infernal flames searing her lips. She looked as though an ancient foe had resurfaced from the pit of her psyche to taunt her once more. She believed she had buried her emotions for Vanessa, that she was over her, but watching her weep in agony was all it took to push it to the surface at a dizzying pace. She wanted to yell, sob, and kick her desktop out the window right now.

"Something came up, Vanessa...I had to leave...

I'll contact you later...

See you then."

The kill sound then played over Vanessa's black Skype phone. "It's so fucking fantastic," she thought. "I've now managed to irritate Anakin. I'm wondering how much worse this situation will be..."

And yet...it was weird how Catherine had abruptly stopped talking. And what was that, she'd asked earlier? "More than you might ever imagine?" Vanessa had suspected for some time that her closest friend was concealing something from her. So what exactly might that be? In the end, the suspense behind her best friend's abrupt exit, as well as a large tub of Ben & Jerry's chocolate therapy, served to distract her from her problems.

Winter of 2013

Catherine

Catherine and her father were enjoying a special Friday evening dinner together. Her mother and sister had gone out, but she had chosen to sit at home. She looked like she was getting a chill, and the sub-zero conditions outdoors weren't enticing. Instead, she had put on her favorite sweatpants and was having a peaceful moment with her father.

"What are you, Catherine? How's it going at university?"

"Uh...Fine...Fine...I'm on my last sprint..."

"Have you considered doing a college degree?"

"No, not really...yeah, why?"

"So...I have a business trip coming up in London...in the United Kingdom. The corporation has pre-paid for a double bed, and your mother will not be accompanying me. But I was curious if you'd want to follow me and look at any colleges there."

"But...but...but...but...but...but...but...but...but Why will I do such a thing? I mean, even though I do find anything fascinating to pursue, how am I supposed to pay for it all? I'm not positive my GPA qualifies for a grant, you see."

"We've talked about it with your mum, Catherine. It's time to spread your wings and fly away from the fold. You're fantastic support around here because you're hardworking, raise your income, and contribute to the household...not to mention that you're..."

Her father seemed to have choked on spaghetti, but Catherine suspected differently. He had a habit of coughing out his emotions while he was upset. It was frowned upon to be less "manly" given the "womenfolk."

"Heh...

I just thought that you're a great business, Catherine, and we enjoy having you in the place. I know that several of your classmates left right after classes, so we appreciate seeing you here. But...and please understand me... I believe it is past time for you to stretch your wings... We've agreed with your mother to arrange for a year of study in the United Kingdom if you so like. Tuition, housing costs, the whole chaos... Please consider it and let us know, OK?"

"Ye, Dad..." Catherine sprang out of her seat and embraced her father before she heard him cough. "I'm at a loss for words...this is...this is daunting!"

"So, worry about it and let me know since we need to buy your airfare, and your visa could take a few days to arrive. My travel is scheduled for three weeks from now... Please consider it and let us know, okay?"

Catherine embraced and kissed her father once more, eliciting a big smile of delight in return. That's just how her father was: rigid granite on the outside, smooth as melting butter on the ground. What was the time? She had to inform Vanessa of the exciting news. Perhaps she should pay her a visit when she is in town. They planned to settle in London, but how far away will Manchester be? Vanessa was doing her internship there as she awaited the start of her graduate program in September.

She was babbling in her head when she went back to her room and turned on her machine. She needed details as soon as possible. And she wanted to tell Vanessa about it.

I read her text and realized I needed to speak to you right away.

I'll be in my apartment in five minutes, c you then.

As she waited for Vanessa, she continued to look at prospective colleges, even though she already knew where she wanted to go. "Let's see...Manchester 1824...hmmm...decent economic department...decent rankings...Warwick is better...Of necessity, the LSE is number one..."

The familiar Skype phone call sound bleeped from her speakers as she scrolled through the different websites. It was, indeed, Vanessa who dialed the number. As she pressed the green "accept video call" icon, her famous face appeared on her phone.

"Hello there, lady! You look smoking hot in those sweatpants! Are you working or something?"

"As a matter of truth, I just came in. Know, it's Friday night? There was a problem at the lab... Any cells have obviously run out of calories, and who are you going to call when it's Friday night, and everybody else is still wasted? Sure thing, bring in the lab rat. That's what I mean... By the way, what are you listening to? For a break, it sounds intriguing... What's up with the shite-eating grin?"

"That will be t.A.T.u - All the Things She Said...I'll paste the connection here. Listen to it again later at peak volume...my it's current preference."

"Anakin, you're stalling...

You've got a story to say. I'm sure it's something good...that smile of yours has almost hit your ears..."

"I'm going to the United Kingdom. My father is going on a business trip in three weeks. We'll be in London, but I'm certain I'll be able to pay you a call."

"That's fantastic stuff, Anakin! Of course, you are welcome to come and see me anytime you want! Space is a little tight, but we'll make do! That's fantastic stuff!"

"And that's just the beginning. My father recently informed me that I could begin my quest for a graduate program over there. The people would pay for all of the costs for a year! Can you picture it?"

"Oh, yes, please, please choose Manchester! Could you please? Please and thank you. I'll be in ecstasy all the time; I'll be fine, I'll cook for you, I'll do your laundry... I pledge to give you everything you desire!"

"Are you a chef? Do you do laundry? Do you promise to give me everything I want? Who are you, and what have you done to Vanessa the original?"

"We're not all gourmet chefs like you, my darling, but I've gotten better. But that's beside the issue. Come on over; it'll be a lot of fun! It'll be almost like the old days, Anakin! I pledge to be excellent!"

Catherine broke out laughing when Vanessa placed on her best grin and conjured a halo over her head with her fingertips. Catherine continued her argument after they had both returned from their fits of laughter:

"You made a compelling point. Okay, the first thought that came to mind when my father sprang this on me was to look at the possibilities of going over there to visit you. I've also done a brief search on Manchester University, and the economics department seems to be solid. I'll look about some more, question some of my teachers over here, and see what I can come up with. In any case, I'll probably visit you when we visit my father."

"That's great! I'm sure we'll have a great time if you text or email me the info. Anakin, Anakin! You truly brightened my day! Only thinking of us together again making me want to run up and down with joy!"

"'Let's not get ahead of ourselves, but I'm pleased as well!'

Kay...Mom has arrived...I must depart...

I'll send you an email or text with the specifics as soon as I get them! Greetings!!"

Catherine pushed the destroy button and slid down the stairs to reach her mother and sister. Today was a day to celebrate; she'd begin her knowledge questionnaire the next day, she reasoned.

Vanessa

Vanessa was pacing back and forth across platforms six and seven of Manchester's Piccadilly train station. She had driven early to pick up her mate, a half-hour earlier, to be exact. That was uncharacteristic of her; punctuality was not her strong suit. Yet she was thrilled to see Anakin, and her positive mood couldn't be ruined for something. They hadn't been able to chat over the Christmas break, what with the normal relative celebrations and getting to see every single one of her friends for just a bit. She was ecstatic about her best friend's visit, and even the distant prospect of Catherine joining her in Manchester left her giddy and lightheaded with delight.

Finally, after thirty minutes of abusing her phone and dismissing the numerous male looks she got, the red Virgin train pulled into the station. Catherine's carriage should be...right in front of her if her knowledge is accurate. She began searching the disembarking passengers nervously, and...there she was! She wore a red and white striped blouse with a matching red cardigan over a pair of tight-casual pants. Her outfit was finished with light brown Converse sneakers. Catherine had never been a fashion slut in her life, but it seemed to Vanessa that she had made a concerted attempt to look beautiful. Was there a smidgeononononononononononononononononononononon on

"Hello there!"

Catherine smiled when she approached her and rushed to embrace her.

"Hello there, lady! It's great to see you! And, by the way, what did you say earlier? What's up?"

"Oh, that's all local slang for hello."

Catherine burst out laughing. "What's up? It sounds completely out of place."

"You have to be patient with me here...this is my fourth year on the island...you can't help but pick up any of the mannerisms. E.g., we'll go to a vodka bar I know later tonight. It'll be awesome!"

"Wicked in the context of a wicked weasel?"

"Wicked in the sense of awesome, cool, wonderful, and fabulous. Anakin, welcome to England. It's great to see you! So...I guess we can first go drop off your bags at my flat...er...apartment...and then go out for a bite to eat."

"That sounds like a good idea to me; I'm hungry."

They walked hand in hand to the bus stop, catching up on each other's lives as they went. Soon after, the double-decker bus arrived and whisked them away to a stop very close to Vanessa's house. The sign above the protection post read, "Emerald Gardens." Well, it was surely surrounded by enough of greenery to deserve the title, Catherine reasoned.

The gate buzzed open after Vanessa swiped her entrance code. She came to a halt in front of the gatehouse and waved to the guard.

"Good evening, Alan."

"Miss Duval, good evening. As usual, you look stunning."

"Alan, you're such a blatant flatterer. This is my friend Catherine, who will be living with me for a few days. Could you please record her in the visitor's logbook for me?"

"That will suffice. Miss, have a good time during your visit."

"You're such a sweetheart. Hello and good day!"

Catherine's eyes opened when she realized what was going on. "Did you label him a cereal?"

"No way, dummy. Cheerio as in farewell, have a nice one, and so forth. As previously said, this is my fourth year on the island. I'm starting to notice colloquialisms. So, shall we proceed then?" Vanessa spoke with a pronounced local accent throughout the last few sentences.

They found their way to Vanessa's apartment. It was essentially a three-bedroom apartment, each with its private bathroom and a communal kitchen and dining space. Vanessa's space was cramped, but she had a wide window with a view of the backyard.

"...Kay...right now...

You'll sleep in my room, and I'll sleep on the floor with this mattress. We should have slept on the same bunk, but as you can see, it's tremendous, and they have a tradition of putting drawers under beds here. Since I twist and switch in my sleep, one of us must have ended up on the floor pretty hard in the middle of the night. That's not cool."

I wouldn't mind dropping off a cliff if it meant sleeping with you, Catherine realized, but she didn't dare to say it aloud. "Maybe I should take the stairs, Vanessa; I feel guilty about kicking you out of your own room," she says instead.

"That is nonsense! It's not every day that I get guests, and you're no regular one. So relax and enjoy your visit. Now...on to business: I suggest we adjust, go to dinner, and then, if your luck holds and we don't get rained on for the night, I'll take you to my favorite Vodka bar, the Revolution. Show you how we celebrate in this region of the country."

They started changing their clothes after deciding on a schedule for the rest of the day.

"Is it you, Leia? What kind of place are we heading after that? What do I wear?"

"Smart casual can suffice. Is it a six-pack you're holding? You've been exercising, haven't you? Girl, you're smoking hot."

Catherine blushed when she noticed blood on her cheeks. "Thank you so much. It's nothing at all, and it's nothing like yours. Last year, I began running long distances. If I'm able, I'd like to run a half-marathon in the future."

"Your body has certainly sexed up a notch. Some guy is going to thank his lucky stars one day..."

Catherine frowned tiredly. "I wonder if I'll ever find the unique person..."

"They should be lined up at your door the way you pose, baby. You simply ought to search around further. Take your nose out of the book, take off your glasses, and they'll just...float to you."

"But I don't think so...

What I want is...

Well, forget about it..."

Vanessa stared at her companion, puzzled. Again, she had the impression that Catherine was concealing something, although she couldn't pinpoint what it was. She wanted to put it aside for the time being. They finished their dressing in complete silence before walking to the restaurant Vanessa had selected for their dinner. The "Pataliputra" was a traditional Indian restaurant on Wilmslow Road, which was also recognized as the "curry mile" because of the high concentration of Pakistani, Indian, and other Asian restaurants.

They began to peruse the menu until they were comfortable. "Now, Anakin, I know you like spicy cuisine, but this place serves the real thing. See how many red peppers there are next to each dish? Anything more than two peppers is a recipe for disaster. So I recommend that we order the naan bread, a platter of egg-fried rice, and a jug of mango lassi in addition to our main courses. It should be more than enough for two. Oh, and a glass of wine if you'd like."

Vanessa went with the chicken tikka sizzler, while Catherine went with the chicken tikka Madras, despite the warnings. They began with a glass of white wine. Vanessa suggested after they clinked their glasses:

"To long-lasting bonds and best mates. Let us hope you get to come over and realize your dreams. Let's only hope we'll be able to work together again."

They sipped their wine and started to converse until their main courses came. Vanessa's bowl was practically on fire, and the waiter extinguished them as he served the pan. Catherine's chicken floats in a deep red sauce that seems to be harmless.

"Wait a minute! You have to ta..."

"Haaaaaaaaaaaaaaaaaaaaaaaaaaaaaaaaaaaaaaaaaaaaaa It's on! BURN!! FUCKING HEAVEN!! The element of water! WINE!"

Catherine's mask had become blood red. Vanessa was in stitches, her eyes welling up with tears from laughing.

"No, here, don't drink wine, drink this," she said, handing over a bottle of mango lassi. "It's yogurt-based, which tends to cool things out. If you don't like it, we will get you a bowl of plain yogurt."

"No, no...everything is perfect. This tastes very well. It's my world! What in the world was that? My tongue was numb!"

"I advised you not to choose it. My friend once ordered the Vindaloo chicken, which is labeled with four peppers. After that, he couldn't feel his tongue for a couple of hours. However, there are a few nefarious things you can do about these... I once offered a blow job after consuming this...it wasn't well-received... I'm curious why."

"If I went down on you, you'd understand why."

"Oh...nooooooooooo...

You naughty little thing! You didn't mention it right now! I'm sure you'd be fine with or without the spices."

Catherine got more intense all of a sudden. She sent Vanessa a strange look but didn't mention anything else.

"It...it was just a prank, Anakin..."

"Uh...oh, yeah..."

"But you did remind me of Tom Hanks in Cast Away as he managed to light the fire...fire, FIRE!"

They continued their chat, finishing their meal in style. The bottle of wine had vanished by the time they left, leaving them both a little drunk.

The "Revolution" was an upscale bar chain. They were going to see in the Deansgate Locks area; it was a collection of railway arches that had been transformed to different commercial uses. The place was truly first-rate for the city; it was once rumored that it was frequented by David Beckham and Victoria Spice's likes while they were in town.

"Right...do you have your passport?"

"Yes...but what are we going to use it for?"

"Everyone under the age of twenty-five must be identified. The venue policy."

"Are you certain we'll make it inside? This position seems to be very wealthy."

"Just take a deep breath, Anakin. Don't worry; you're with me now."

Two massive bouncers guarded the entry to the bar with necks wider than their shoulders. They were dressed to the nines, complete with headpieces, and they were positively terrifying. But then Vanessa simply grinned at them, they laughed, and they were ushered in with no questions asked.

"You never stop to astound me, do you? I won't ask if those two know you because I don't want to know."

"We like to please Miss Blickman; we just want to please her. What is your poison of preference for tonight?"

"Whatever you're getting, I guess...I'm not very knowledgeable about hard liquor..."

"Then Absolute pepper vodka would suffice. I normally drink mine straight, but because we've already had our wine and you're a featherweight, I'll order them with tomato juice."

Only a few sips; they were both feeling the effects of the buzz.

"So...what about that sexy blonde man over there? He's been swallowing you with his eyes since we walked in."

"I'm not your kind."

"Catherine, please! He's got sex on his legs! So, what is your personality type?"

"Could we kindly refrain from beating a dead horse? He's not my style, and I'm not in the mood for a one-night stand. In reality, I've never had one and would never have one. That's not how I roll."

"Have you been on a date since I left?"

"No, Vanessa...I would have told you, all right?"

"However, why?"

Catherine exasperatedly glanced at her closest mate. "You're not going to let this go, are you?" She chugged her drink and slammed her glass on the wooden stand quite loudly, not anticipating a response. "Can I please get another?"

"Uhh...sure...are we all right here?"

"I'll be there until you get me another one. And...forget about the tomato juice this time."

Vanessa returned with two double pepper vodkas on the rocks in her lap. Catherine took a large sip from her drink, put it down, and without looking at her mate...

"I'm bisexual, Vanessa."

Catherine

She stood there watching as her friend almost choked on her soda. "What exactly are you? Why is this so? I say, how?"
Catherine gave a sad face. "Vanessa, there is no how or why. They are the cards that have been dealt with me; I did not choose them... It's not because I awoke one day thinking, "How do I make my life more miserable?" Oh, I know...why don't I become a dyke!"

"But...but, you nutcase, why didn't you tell me...

I'm afraid not...

I've been awful, haven't I? I mean...I've been hounding you and attempting to hook you up for years... I'm feeling bad right now..."

"I...I didn't say because I was afraid...I am afraid...of losing you..."

"What are you on about? You're my greatest buddy in the whole universe. This is the year 2013, not the Stone Age. Nobody cares who you want to sleep with. YOU ARE MY MOST VALUED FRIEND! Whatever the case might be! Now, I've been a lousy friend in the past, and God only knows how much unnecessary psychological burden I've placed you under, but I'm still here, sister. You're not going to get rid of me that quickly."

Catherine's cheeks were smeared with tears. "Thank you...you have no idea how much this means to me..." she said shakily.

Vanessa encircled her closest friend in a bear embrace. "Do you want to leave? Let's just take a stroll back to my apartment. We ought to get the alcohol out of our bodies."

They had left the bar and were on their way back to Vanessa's flat in a matter of minutes. The crisp winter breeze felt amazing on their ears, and it was cool to talk without having to yell.

"So...err...since when...you know...have you been...have you been...have you known?"

"Let's just claim I've always had a soft spot for the female type. Keep in mind that this would not often imply a sexual manner. I don't walk down the street and say, "Wow, great boobs, nice pussy, I want to bang her." While I was younger, I used to have crushes...you know, childish things...on our second-grade instructor, our skating coach, and other such people. When our hormones kicked in, I was perplexed... perplexed. I figured I was crazy before I began reading about it. For the very least, I realized I wasn't alone in the universe.

And I went through a disbelief phase...you know, this can't be happening to me, it's just a phase...it'll pass. If you recall, that's when I tried my hand at dating. I figured, against my better judgment, that if I found the right one, maybe this thing...would go away. I attempted...I..."

Vanessa gently snatched Catherine's hand and squeezed her. Still, tears streamed down her cheeks; it was a silent, agonizing scream.

"You're not needed to do this, sweetie..."

"No...I've hidden this stuff inside me for so long that I worried I'd lose my mind. I have plenty to teach you...I have to tell you..."

"Catherine, Catherine, Catherine...

I wish there were a way to alleviate any of your suffering, boy."

Catherine exchanged a lonely expression with Vanessa. "I so wish you could... Anyway, as I previously said, I experimented with dating... I did a lot of dumb stuff. Vanessa, I'm not a virgin... Joaquin and I had sex... If you have some recollection of him? We were about to enter twelfth grade at the time. You were all on my case at the time, so I said, what the hell...I went out with him that summer... Kissing him feels like kissing cardboard, not like the stars and wonder you all mentioned."

Vanessa's expression had changed to that of curiosity. "You little sassy! You never mentioned it! That's what I have no idea about!"

"Because you had the long trip with your family to Spain over the summer, your antennae didn't pick it up. No, wait, there's more... I had intercourse with him twice...it was awful... I didn't have any feelings... Fortunately, amid my suffering, Joaquin proved to be a true gentleman when I begged him to stay friends simply. He didn't put some burden on me...perhaps he knew that I wasn't really into him or anything. Still, luckily, he was calm...extremely calm. After that...

"...after which I had sex with a child. It was the summer before you left for the UK, and we were on a camping trip together. Do you remember Olivia? You kept trying to hook me up every night, and I kept making excuses until one night I grabbed Olivia, who seemed similarly desperate or lonely, and we ran away. Olivia, it turns out, played both sides of the fence, and what began as a scalp massage ended...errrmmmm...well...you know..."

"You're blushing, Catherine...what more am I going to learn and see today for the first time?"

"Stop talking, Vanessa...anyway, when you were occupied with Mr. Insecurity that summer, I had a lot of...encounters with Olivia. She was a good person, but she made it plain that we were just having a fling. But she did, in a way, open my mind..."

"...and don't even get me started on your thighs..."

"Hahahahahahahahahahahahahahahahahahahahahahahah ahahahahahahahahahahahahaha So, to get into the specifics, the sex was fantastic, and there was this light-bulb moment inside my brain, like, soooooo...this is how it's meant to feel..."

Meanwhile, they had arrived at Vanessa's house without even realizing it. Neither girl was in the mood for sleep, so they resumed their conversation while sitting on Vanessa's bunk.

"...so...how is the sex...?

I know, there's a ton of oral and all, but what else?"

Catherine blushed again for the second time that night.
"You uuuuuuuuuuuuuuuuuuuuuuuuuuuuuuuuuuuuuuuuuuuuuu uuuuu It's not too dissimilar to hetero genders. Yes, there is a lot of oral, and certainly, fingers are involved...as are dolls, if you're into that kind of stuff, although I've never used any. I tend to be truthful in my tongue and hands. Then there's Tribbing, which can be just incredible."

"Err...since I don't have my lesbian dictionary at the moment, what exactly is Tribbing?"

"Well...scissoring? You know...when you rub your..."

"I'm blushinggg..."

"Oh for fuck's shake...when it's you brush pussies on each other. That's what I'm going to say about it. Are you happy now?"

"And...how does it feel?"

"Fuck yeah...God, Olivia was so...so fine at this..."

Catherine noticed Vanessa's eyes were glistening. There was a tangible tension entering the space, a gravity-like power that began to close the gap between them. Catherine's gaze was fixed on Vanessa's profile, her eyes closed and her lips slightly apart. "Oh my God...going she's to embrace me...we're going to kiss...is this going to happen? It's not possible! I'll clarify more..."

They were shocked and jumped to the ceiling when they saw a big crash next door.

"Wait, what was that?"

"Oh, that's just my cretin next-door neighbor pounding on his door. Any time he does it, it makes my skin crawl. Do you like a cup of tea? I'm heading to the kitchen to make one for myself. If you're interested, I still have some chamomile."

"No, I'm fine, thank you. Shouldn't we, like, cover the beds first? As a result..."

"Oh, yeah, definitely...um...yeah...right...so...beds first...tea next...or no tea..."

"Greetings, Vanessa! Just relax, please. It never took place. Take it easy!"

Vanessa exhaled an audible breath of relaxation. "Oh my God...I'm so happy...because...friendship...but...I'm glad you're cool about it."

"It never did, as I previously said. Deal? You go get the tea, and I'll prepare the beds."

Vanessa

It had been two weeks after Catherine had quit, and it was now Friday evening. The weather outside was changing between sleet and rain, with a cold northern wind blowing. They were expecting a couple of inches of snow later that night, according to the prediction. How will Vanessa be bothered by the snow? She grew up in a place where five or six months of snowfall was the standard of any winter. What she despised were the constant overcast and the erratic rainfall. And, indeed, rain fell in all forms in northwestern England. Showers, drizzles, sleet, proper rain, downpour rain, tiny droplet-rain-like little icicles, the kind that soaked you down to your clothes.

She began exploring the ether realm because she was bored to tears. For some strange explanation, the term "Tribbing" came to mind; the same one Catherine had used to explain lesbian sex to her that night. She checked for it on Google and received thousands of results. The pictures she obtained were stills from pornographic films, some of which were gross yet extremely provocative. "So that's how it's handled," she thought as she readjusted a wedged section of her panties casually. She then typed in "female kissing" and scrolled through a plethora of stunning pictures.

"What about...hmmm...lesbian movies? Let's see what that elicits, "She pondered. "Is there a room in Rome? I'm curious what that's all about." She opened the film's overview by clicking on the YouTube page.

In what seems to be an innocent romantic experience crowning their last night in Rome, Alba (Elena Anaya) seduces an outsider Natasha (Natasha Yarovenko) to her hotel room (the specifics of how they met in a club are left vague). Tentatively, the two bond profoundly through a weave of stories, genders, memories, and interaction with artworks in the space, delving deeper and deeper into the depths of reality, trust, and, eventually, affection. The couples mutually consent to split up, moving to their former lives in Russia and Spain.

Vanessa sat back in her chair, intrigued and pressing play. She observed as the film played out in front of her eyes; it was nothing like the crappy porn that some of her boyfriends had shown her in an attempt to entice her into a threesome. This sounded naughty and erotic at the same moment. As she stood there watching, she felt a familiar swelling in her nether zone, followed by a flurry of butterflies in the lower section of her stomach. Her weight shifting on her chair didn't stop the increasing tide, but she decided to forget her simmering arousal for the time being.

But when the film got to the bath sequence, her desire became much stronger. Two amazingly gorgeous females were feverishly hugging and petting inside a water-filled bathtub right in front of her.

She rose from her chair and sprawled on her bed as the closing credits rolled through her television. She was also extremely horny and incredibly interested. Questions would have to wait; her carnal desires would have to take precedence for the time being. She drew in her breath and lowered her side, closing her eyes. Her skin was burning when the cotton material of her t-shirt made contact with it. Her hand moved closer to her, pleading for love, pussy as her mind flashed back to the film she had just watched.

Her sluggish left hand groped at her C-cup breast, not wanting to be left out of the fight. Her erect nipple was almost painfully rubbed with her tee when she used a mix of hefty pulls, caresses, and pinches to heighten her satisfaction. The main course, though, was being eaten elsewhere; soon, her vagrant hand had crossed under the waistline of her sweatpants and panties and made contact with her pubic hair. Slowly descending, it scaled the heights of her mons pubis before delectably plunging through the space behind her lips.

Never before had Vanessa felt such a strong need to dip her fingertips in her wetness. She didn't just dip; she rammed one and then two digits inside her, mashing her clitoris with her hand the whole time as her fingertips withdrew and reinserted themselves, images of nude girls embracing and touching played through her head.

Her heightened sense of desire couldn't be met with those restricted tactics, so sweat pants were kicked off, and panties were tossed aside in a futile attempt to supply her hand with further control. She rolled onto her side and curled into a fetal position, her fingertips trapped within her sopping pussy lips.

Vanessa was overcome with an intoxicating combination of intense arousal and desperation; she couldn't recall ever having to contend with such greed. Her arousal had been simmering under the surface for some time, and now that the ballast had been blown, it was racing towards the surface at a breakneck pace. As her point and index fingers swished across her enlarged clitoris, her hand picked up in rhythm. Her breathing became shallow when her orgasm approached, and she felt hot flashes course across her body. As her hand picked up the pace, she let out a short, gentle moan.

And her thoughts flashed back to someone kissing her as she laid crouched on her bunk. Illusionary hands appeared and roamed all over her body. "Oh yes...yes...Oh God, yes..." she said in hushed tones. Imaginary lips brushed her flesh and pulled on her breasts, bringing joy beams through all four corners of her body. And then there was a smile; the unseen perpetrator produced by her imagination had a face, and it was...Catherine!

And that was the straw that broke the camel's back for Vanessa. The build-up to her climax felt monumental, and the ecstasy that followed was explosive. Her thighs clamped down tightly on her hand as her whole body stiffened. She let out a long "aaaaahhhh" as she felt the walls of her vagina pulsate with pleasure. It just kept going... and going... and going... and going... and going... and going... and going... The rubbing of her palm would hold her climax going only as she felt it was done. After a solid minute of riding this phenomenal wave of ecstasy, her body collapsed on the mattress, and she passed out where she laid.

A couple of hours later, the chill in her room and the wet patch on her bed cover woke her up. Vanessa giggled as she stretched luxuriously on her bed; her body looked incredibly comfortable and renewed. The very thought of her climax sent delightful tingles down her neck.

"Well...that was one for the books...can't recall ever seeing a great one." She smirked at the idea. She had necked and petted three boyfriends and been exclusive with two since she began dating. Her first long-distance engagement had been with Nicholas, and now she was in another with Percy. But none of them had ever offered her such a good time. In reality, come to think of it, only Percy had sent her a couple of bad ones, which shocked her.

Until that stage, she had assumed she was "one of those ladies" who couldn't orgasm by intercourse. Intercourse had been slightly pleasurable for her; in retrospect, her orgasms with a lover had occurred when Percy had grudgingly gone down on several occasions. And Vanessa wasn't a regular masturbator; she felt it was disrespectful to her boyfriends to do so, and on other events, she couldn't be bothered. In this case, though, she came strong and fast; there was no doubt about it. And she'd been attracted and orgasmed by female photographs, fantasizing about her best friend no less. Did that have any impact on her?

"Naaaaaaaaaaaaaaaaaaaaaaa

I suppose it's just a lack of sex...

I had to be hornier than I realized...

I'll take the train tomorrow and pay Percy a surprise visit...

That should clear stuff up..."

Summer of 2013

Catherine

Catherine stood at the kitchen table with her sister and parents for breakfast on a lazy Sunday morning.

"So, have you decided on a curriculum yet? Have you received any acceptances?"

"Well, yes...in truth, I've received three acceptance letters...one from the University of Edinburgh, one from Manchester, and one from the London School of Economics."

"Wow, young lady! What is the LSE? That seems like a huge deal, doesn't it?"

"Yeah, it's first in the UK and seventh in the world, but yeah...as far as economies go, it's a huge deal. There is one minor caveat, however: their tuition rates are out of this world. We're talking about thirty-eight to thirty-nine thousand dollars alone for tuition, not to mention the cost of living in London, which, based on what I've heard, is worse than Toronto."

"Yeah...38 thousand is a little too much for us, love..."

"I know, and I wasn't going to ask...you guys are already too kind, so I don't want to feel selfish or anything. To be frank, I've settled for Manchester."

"Oh? Why is this so? Edinburgh is said to be a lovely place to research. Doesn't Manchester seem a little drabber?"

"Well...ermm...the department in Manchester is rated higher, and their tuition rates are more reasonable, ranging between thirteen and fourteen thousand pounds...

Vanessa has already begun her Ph.D. studies there. She's been there for years...she'll teach me the ropes so I can adjust faster.

Plus, seeing a mate in a new location is still a plus... So, well, I'm leaning that way...I guess I'll agree if you don't mind."

Her father turned to face her mother; they were having their normal silent talk, which comes from years of loving each other. Her mother nodded, and the debate was over. Her request will be accepted.

She excused herself from the kitchen table and dashed upstairs to her place. She had a lot on her plate; she had to respond to the graduate student's office email and fill out the electronic form for student residence. She needed to make a rough estimate of her estimated living expenses to provide to her parents. Most importantly, she had to inform Vanessa of the good news.

Once again, Skype was going to be the medium by which she will share her joy. Vanessa was online, and after a few seconds, her famous face filled the frame of her laptop. However, the familiar face was marred by puffy red eyes and dark circles the Oreo cookies' size.

"Errrr...Leia? Are you okay, girl? You ought to have been hit in the chest."

"More than certainly, he stabbed me in the back. Remember how I told you about my unexpected visit to Percy two weeks after you left?"

"Are you sure?"

"What I didn't tell you was that I met a flustered and disheveled girl in his flat's standard room...and a few seconds later, I met an almost panicked Percy in his room. When I confronted him about the girl or why he was acting strangely, he stammered something about being sick. At the time, I decided to dismiss my thoughts and chalk it up to him being under the weather.

But yesterday, when I repeated the routine and paid him a surprise visit, the girl was there again...only this time I caught her in his room...scantily clad...

Then I informed him we were finished and walked away...bloody bastard..."

"Oh, poor me...I'm so sorry, Leia...I'm at a loss for words..."

"Oh, please screw him...he was crap in bed anyway...and he was cheating on me behind my back, so fuck him...

It's just that...you anticipate a little more honesty from somebody you've been dating for almost two years...we began off, so differently, then it all had to finish this way. Just develop some goddamn balls and tell me, you asshole, there's no reason to go behind my back! Jesus Christ! What did I do wrong to end up with all these mentally ill people?"

"There's nothing wrong with you...

You're only aiming in the wrong direction...sometimes happiness is right in front of you, so near that we don't see it."

"Oh? What exactly does it imply?"

"Nothing in particular...

I'm certain you'll meet the guy of your dreams... this stuff happens when you least anticipate them."

"So, how are you? Is there a pretty girl bound to your bedpost over there?"

Catherine blushed visibly, which never ceased to delight Vanessa. "What are you talking about? Don't tell me you have no one... Any fortunate lady must be involved. You're gorgeous, witty, funny, and the greatest girl ever... I'd completely do you if I were into ladies."

Catherine coughed as she swallowed. On the other end of the line, Vanessa had thought about her suffering and was smiling for the first time in a long time. "Relax, baby... I forgot how simple it is to pull your rope."

"Straight up, straight up, straight up, straight up, straight up, straight up, mixed up, straight up, straight up, straight up

You wouldn't be joking if I held you in bed with me. More than certainly, you'd be yelling!"
"Promises promises...a lot of smoke but no flames!"
"Isn't it true that your mother taught you not to play with fire? What are you talking about? If you want to take a walk on the wild side right now?"
"Who knows...there could be a couple of twists in the lane," Vanessa teased.

But this was no longer a game that Catherine wanted to enjoy. Vanessa was only teasing her, but as her previous visit had shown, it just took the smallest thing for her emotions to spiral out of reach. Was studying in Manchester the best decision?

Was she acting in the best interests of her family? Yes, she will react to herself. Given the limitations, it was the best choice for her research. Vanessa was her mate first and foremost. Despite her frivolity and the previous occurrence, she was certain she was as straight as an arrow. She wasn't, wasn't she?

"Anyway...aside from the crooked tracks, that's not why I named you. I've taken place in Manchester... Until anything unexpected happens, I'll be visiting there in September."

Vanessa began shouting into her microphone, which was picked up as screeching in Catherine's headphones. "Ohmygodohmygodohmygodohmygodohmygodohmygodohmyg odohmy Anakin, Anakin! That's fantastic stuff! We're going to have a wonderful time together! It would be almost like the old days! I'll have you on tour! We'll go out as a group! We're going shopping! We'll do..."

"Hold your horses, boss. First and foremost, nothing has been finalized. I said I'd consider their bid, but it's contingent on my final grades here...which I'm sure about... Then what? Partying? What kind of partying? According to what I've seen, the course is meant to be brutal. Plus, my parents are going to pay a small fortune... Over there, I'm going to have to train like a madman."

"Yesyesyesyesyesyesyesyesyesyesyesyesyesyesyesyes You have no idea how pleased you just got me! And...ehem...Anakin, I pledge to be nice! I guarantee it! Can you see what I mean? I've fashioned an angelic halo above my head!"

Catherine couldn't help but grin as she saw Vanessa's spectacular mood swing. Wow, it will be wonderful to see her closest friend again. If she could only hold her heart in place...

Autumn of 2013

Vanessa

Vanessa had a feeling of déjà vu as she waited for Catherine's flight to arrive at Manchester's international airport. She had landed way ahead of schedule and was pacing restlessly across the lobby stores, attempting to dispel her nervousness. That was another odd occurrence for her; she was almost always in full control and was not fazed about something. And while she was a couple of hours out from her period, which couldn't be avoided. But what was the source of her trepidation? It was more likely attributed to the joy of actually seeing Catherine come over for good. "Oh boy...A whole year with Anakin..." she thought to herself, laughing.

Lifting her head, she looked at the arrivals monitors and her watch. Yes, a Lufthansa flight from Frankfurt has just landed. It was now only a matter of waiting for twenty minutes or so. In any event, she'd be laden with baggage. Oh right, thank goodness for smartphones. She attempted to read her Facebook wall but couldn't concentrate. She threw the phone into her pocket and proceeded to the arrivals gate where Catherine would appear. Passengers began to exit through the frosted glass window, but her companion was nowhere to be seen and until...a pair of hands gripped her eyes.

"Can you guess who?"

"Anakin!" exclaimed the narrator.

Vanessa spun around and bear-hugged her mate, almost tackling her to the ground.

"Take it simple, there, baby! I'm glad to see you as well!"

"I'm...just...overjoyed to see you, Anakin! And you have the appearance of a zombie child. Is it just that horrible of a flight?"

"The flight was fine, but it was quite long. I couldn't find a direct flight, and the connection to Heathrow was $200 more expensive, so I went via Frankfurt, which added a couple more hours. I believe I'm already in the air. My legs are a little shaky, so I'll get by. So, what's the game plan?"

"So, first and foremost, we take both of these suitcases and unload them at my apartment. Then, if you're interested, we can go to the student housing office. Yes, they've reserved you for my place of residence, so it's a first-come, first-served basis. If we're fortunate, we could wind up living in the same apartment. So you must get there as fast as possible. It's the best way to ensure a good location."

They had the opportunity to catch up on their taxi ride. Vanessa filled her in on the gory facts about Percy's infidelity and how she had eventually dumped him.

"...and that was the end of the loser, and not too much. How are you? Did you manage to land a girl in your lap?"

"No, not at all...

Under any scenario, I would have informed you about it. I've been on a few dates, but little has come of them. Do keep in mind that I've maintained a low profile back home...I mean, yeah, I did come out to my parents, and thank God, it went well...in truth, it went impossibly well compared to some of the horror stories I've read about. But, in either case, no...no long-term partnership."

"Oh...okay...the what's deal with the rainbow lapel pin on your bag?"

"Hey, that's me announcing to the rest of the planet that I'm homosexual...

Vanessa, I've chosen to turn the tab. To step out of my shell...to be more outgoing and not mask my true self. And that little rainbow is my first teeny-tiny move in that direction."

"I can tell you've improved, Anakin, and in a positive way. I hope that this new beginning gives you everything you want. I...er...I have a little welcome present for you. I wasn't going to tell you about it, but you know me...can't keep this stuff hidden...anyway, I'll send it to you when we get to my house."

"Awwww...you can be such a softie at times...you mean you have a present...what is it?"

"Nope...you're not going to get any further details from me."

"Well, I suppose I might tickle you..."

Vanessa's eyes were packed with mock horror. "No, Anakin...no, Anakin...ha-ha...no...come on...you realize I'm ticklish...we're...we're...stop...we're in a cab...what will the cabbie think?"

"...I think he'd find it hot to see you all red and flustered..." Catherine bent over and whispered in her ear.

Vanessa felt electric sparks shoot down her spine with every word Catherine said in her ears. Her nipples hardened, and her skin became prickly all over. Why was she having such an influence on her? She recalled their almost-kiss the night Catherine had visited her, preceded by her self-love session two weeks later after Room in Rome.

Blushing was not in her arsenal, but she blushed when she responded: "eeeeeeeeeeeeeeeeee

I'm certain he will...

Are you hungry or something? If you want something to eat? I have macaroni and cheese baked in the oven. If you like, we should nuke it and then go look through your applications..."

Catherine

It had been a long and exhausting day for Catherine, but Vanessa had been correct: arriving early at the student housing office had paid off handsomely. Despite not getting a space in Vanessa's apartment, she ended up in an all-female dorm with five other roommates. Her window overlooked the garden and pond, and Vanessa's apartment was just a few stairs down.

She rubbed her eyes to remain open and avoided falling to her bed because she realized it would just make her more jet-lagged in the morning. Instead, she spent her days sorting her emotions and storing her clothing. This was her first time away from college, and she was looking forward to it. Vanessa had told her that the "blues" might begin to strike her about a month later in the game, but they may not. Catherine's overseas "adventure," as she called it, had been planned until she was older and more experienced. She had done so with much consideration, not on the spur of the moment. She still didn't have any romantic interests back home to wish for.

In reality, when it came to partnerships, Vanessa's odd behavior was her most significant question mark so far. There seemed to be specific kinks in her straightness. Or it may just be her overactive imagination. She had to confess that Vanessa never blushed or ran out of vocabulary. True, her "whispering" had been more than mere fun, but her friend had responded like a deer trapped in headlights, rather than merely laughing it off with a glib comment of her own.

Again, the sensible portion of her brain blinked serious warning lights; pursuing a straight girl or a girl who lived a sober life was a prescription for catastrophe. Going for your straight best friend was equivalent to committing mental suicide. At best, Vanessa would be intrigued by girl-on-girl amorous interaction; they'd share a romp in the hay once or twice, Catherine might get physically committed, and then Vanessa might tell her that she couldn't do it, that she wanted to remain buddies, and so on. Catherine knew this would shatter her heart into a million fragments. Was she able to put herself in that position? It was the most disturbing thinking of them all: she didn't know the response to that issue.

September came and went, and with it, the harsh truths of a doctoral program surfaced. Catherine had twelve hours of taught classes a week and four hours of exercise solving sessions under tutelage. Her professors moved at a breakneck pace and assumed a full understanding of the mathematical methods available. Reading suggested journal articles were not only welcomed but, in certain cases, needed. To her dismay, Catherine discovered that correctly addressing a query or experimenting was no longer sufficient. To shine, you had to take the initiative to utilize various outlets. In a way, this meant putting in long hours of study and analysis.

Vanessa was still knee-deep in work for her Ph.D., and she often worked twelve-hour shifts at her study. She didn't get to see her too much, which was probably just as well because she wanted to concentrate right now. Catherine took to the road to clear her head and unwind; she would sprint for ten to twelve kilometers three days a week and swim fifteen hundred meters at the university swimming pool another two. Her body had finally begun to grow up beautifully, and for the first time in her life, she felt incredibly confident of herself as she looked in the mirror at her idol.

Then, in the middle of all her coursework, she encountered Nora, a lovely Spanish girl with whom she shared some of her lessons. Nora possessed a dark Mediterranean complex, lined with dark brown curly hair and skin. She was shorter than her, but she had killer curves and a big bust. It was her tiny rainbow lapel that did the trick; Nora had spotted it and asked her about it. One event leads to another, and they wound up going to the student union for a cup of coffee.

Nora turned out to be bisexual, much like herself, and she secretly expressed her curiosity in her. Catherine was flattered, but she wasn't sure whether she desired an amorous engagement during her graduate studies. She did, however, plan to go on another date with her; there was nothing wrong with going out with another gay girl. You might say and feel something that your straight friend would find challenging to comprehend, for one example. Things that, in her situation, you'd never tell your closest friend about.

Vanessa

It had been a normal gloomy Friday evening, with freezing rain falling all day. Vanessa had tried to avoid lab duties that evening and had contacted Catherine to see if she wanted to head out with her. They had hemmed and hawed for a time before settling on the pub right next to their hall of residence.

The Flaming Lion was your average British restaurant. It looked like I was entering an old home. There were many sitting rooms with polished wooden tables and benches and a large rounded bar in the center that offered an array of tap beers, wines, and spirits. There were some large old-style windows in each wall, and there was also a glass-enclosed sunroom. Outside was a green garden of wooden benches and tables on the occasional days when the weather permitted sitting outside. Overall, the mood was relaxed and upbeat. They could be partying in one room while watching a football game or playing Trivial Pursuit in the other.

Both girls were dressed comfortably in leggings and hoodies; they weren't out for a major night out, only a beer and a catch-up conversation. Vanessa chose a pint of Guinness, while Catherine chose Carling.

"So...long time, no see...how are you doing so far?"

"Ugh...been it's a little hectic so far. I'll give them that the course is very challenging. Math is indeed a big part of my life. In reality, I'm not sure why they bothered assigning our courses different titles. Math I, II, III, and IV should have sufficed."

"Yes, it was like this for me as well. Taught graduate courses are very difficult...it should get simpler for you after the first exams. The second semester normally has a variety of electives because you can choose and select anything you want."

"So, how have you been? I haven't seen you in a long time."

"Hmmm...what shall I say? Nightmarish isn't quite near. My boss pays for both my education and my monthly salary, so expectations are strong. We're now working on a report about mitochondrial matrices...err...the powerhouses of cells... I just need to have this published, or else my Ph.D. will be thrown away, and I'll be offered a buddy MPhil slap on the back...but...enough of this nonsense...just let's forget about university for a bit, shall we? How is your life in general here? Is there anything new? Is there something I should be aware of? Speak up! Your princess has given you orders!"

Catherine grinned and pretended to bow: "Oh, your most illustrious highness...

Let me think about it...

Well, there is something, now that I think about it. But nothing too important... There's this kid in my class...or at least any of my classes. We went out for brunch the other day, and we're heading out for dinner tomorrow."

Vanessa had been chugging a huge mouthful of her beer and had almost choked, attempting to gulp it all down. "Oh, really? And how is she doing? Should I recognize her?" She tried valiantly to sound casual about it, but she was oddly pricked by what she had discovered.

"Her name is Nora, and she's Spanish...as in Spanish, not Latin American...

I suppose she's entertaining to be around...

It's...just it's none..."

"But you're going on a date, so she's got to be relevant."

"I wouldn't go so far as to say it was a date. To be frank, I'm not sure what it is. She was the one who confronted me in the first place. Remember the lapel pin you saw on my bookbag when I first arrived? Oh, she found that as well, and it turns out she's lesbian, so it's great to have someone to speak to."

Vanessa seemed to be in pain. Catherine was the first to remember. "I didn't say it in that sense, Leia... I mean...you know...err...share any stuff with somebody in your squad. I'm not making a lot of sense, am I?"

"No, no...everything is perfect. I understand. One day, this queer chick appears, and I'm instantly obsolete."

"Vanessa.....

I'd claim you were jealous if I didn't know better."

In her pint, Vanessa snorted: "WHAT ABOUT ME? Are you envious? What are you envious of? What am I to be envious of because we have a history? I was so irritated when you suggested you couldn't tell me something that was on your mind."

Catherine glanced at her mate, puzzled, but said nothing. They changed the topic, but Vanessa was not having a good time. After finishing her pint, she pretended to have a headache and recommended that she return early.

"Are you certain? We've just had one pint so far."

"Yeah...I'm sorry for ruining the crowd, but I'm not feeling good. I'm going to take some ibuprofen and try to catch some early z's."

"Do you want me to come to your room? We might watch a video or anything like that..."

"Not today, Anakin...but thank you for your bid."

"Wow...all right...

I'm going to my place...

If you need something, just send me a call, and I'll come over right away."

They returned to their home, and Vanessa waved goodbye with a dry and cold "goodnight." After seeing Catherine's shocked and hurt face, she felt bad about her behavior. Vanessa was furious with herself. What made her so envious? What was the source of this possessiveness? Catherine was a girly kid, while Vanessa was a straight man. She wasn't, wasn't she? If she was, why did she feel like slitting the throat of that Spanish girl? What was her name? She wanted a decent shag, that's it. Had she just spoken the phrase "shag"? She'd wasted much too many years on this forsaken island, and that was the source of her dilemma, she reasoned.

Catherine
For a break, the weather was calm; it was cool, so Catherine didn't mind. In reality, according to what her parents had warned her about the season's first big blizzard, this was summer weather as long as it didn't sprinkle for a change.

Catherine quietly waited outside Nora's house for her; she had arrived early and was walking up and down the driveway, attempting to relax her jittery nerves. Only relax, she told herself; it's just a fun eat-and-drink gathering, isn't it? She argued that she was just heading out with a potential mate.

And Catherine had been doing a lot of reasoning over the last few hours. Vanessa's actions had been odd. She had found it hilarious at first that she could throw such a childish tantrum at her for such insignificant detail. Her actions had hurt her at the time; she had done nothing bad to warrant that punishment. Of course, she had acted equally as Vanessa had regaled her with her passionate trysts. But it was uncharacteristic of her to be jealous; possessive, indeed, but jealous? What are you envious of? Wasn't Vanessa a straight girl? What if she's not? What if she was giving contradictory signals?

Catherine kept calling and messaging Vanessa, but both of her calls and texts were returned. She had considered canceling her date with Nora, but for what reason? Canceling because Vanessa was jealous and there was a one in a million possibility she was interested in her? No way, not in this fairy story, boy. She was heading on a date with Nora, and Vanessa was free to sulk whatever she could. Furthermore, as she had read somewhere, passion can only be forgotten in love. She had a life to live, and she couldn't keep on to childhood crushes forever.

She almost leaped, so engrossed was she in her thoughts, when she noticed a soft touch on her arm.

"Hello, chica, how are you?"

"Uhhhh...very well, and you?"

"Catherine, do you know Spanish? That's a pleasant treat!"

"And that very well sums up my knowledge of spoken Spanish. I briefly took a class during my university years, but I had to abandon it due to job overload...you, by the way, are beautiful..."

And pretty didn't even come close; Nora was clad in a sparkling powder blue stylish hoodie that hugged her body in all the right ways. Her hair was pulled back into a high ponytail, exposing matching stud earrings. She completed her look with dollhouse denim and a pair of black suede Pumas. She was dressing lightly but neatly, and the earrings revealed to Catherine that she had paid attention to detail. That, plus the minimal make-up.

Nora grinned inwardly when she saw Catherine inspecting her. She wanted to get her date back down to earth, coughing softly. "So...you promised to take me out to dinner...where would you like to go? I'm familiar with this Spanish restaurant; they make an excellent paella. Is there something you'd be involved in?"

Catherine could feel the blood on her cheeks. She'd been captured looking, albeit not in a subtle way. But, well, she was just human, and Nora was surely attractive. "Oh, yeah...that'd be cool. I'm a big fan of trying different foods. I've never been to a Spanish restaurant before, so...yeah...I'm up for it."

They boarded the bus and were fortunate to have a double seat available. Nora stood right next to Catherine in the window seat, their hips and legs touching. Catherine noted their proximity and didn't mind a whit. In reality, her body communicated "I like that" in a variety of ways. Nora may have sat farther apart, but she didn't.

The "La Mancha" was a charming Spanish restaurant on Deansgate Street, close to the Instituto Cervantes. The comparatively bland brick outer façade did nothing to acquaint passers-by with the comfortable inside. Catherine was happily surprised by the high ceilings and wood paneling lining the walls as she entered. The room was divided into three sections: one with an expansive bar, another with more private stalls, and the other with large wooden barrels acting as tables.

When Nora entered, she was welcomed and embraced by many people; it was clear that she'd been here before and was well-liked. Nora talked quickly with the hostess in Spanish, and they were promptly escorted to a corner booth that was both large and largely secluded. She graciously let Catherine pick her seat first and then sat across from her.

"So...as our main course, I'd recommend the paella for two. The tapas are served with our beverages first, and if we haven't already filled ourselves to the max, we should try the pastel Cordobes, a dessert from my hometown."

Catherine smiled warmly at her. "That's fantastic! I'm still up for trying different flavors. What are we going to drink?"

"Ideally, we'd have a glass of wine to accompany our meal. The Cune Rioja Rosado, a blush semi-dry juice, should complement our paella perfectly. But if you want a bottle, they have San Miguel on hand, which is also good."

"If you don't mind, I'd like the champagne. I'm not a big wine drinker, but I'd like to give it a shot."

"I was hoping you'd mention anything like that."

Nora smiled brightly, revealing flawless white teeth underneath. Catherine returned the smile; she was such a beautiful person, and the powder blue of her hoodie accentuated her Mediterranean tan perfectly.

Their wine had arrived, and their tongues had been loosened as a result.

"...so...the word Nora...interesting. I'd never learned about it before, even though I had a lot of Latino classmates..."

"So to say, it's not Spanish. If you choose, it's most definitely Moorish or Arabic. It is the feminine version of the Arabic word Noor, which means "light." As you may have inferred from my skin tone, I am from Andalucia, Spain's southernmost region.

During the Middle Ages, my hometown of Cordoba served as the seat of the Cordoba Caliphate. It was a great cultural, educational, and artistic center... Naturally, there were a couple of Arabs or Moors...you might have learned of the term Moriscos. There were citizens of mixed descent, a cross-pollination of Arab and Iberian populations... Anyway, I'm starting to bore you..."

"No way! No way, just continue, "said Catherine, as she carelessly pressed her hand on top of Nora's. "Oh...sorry," she apologized, seeing her blood pressure rise once more.

"Don't be concerned, Catherine. To cut a long story short, my grandmother had this tag, and before her, her grandmother, and so on. We've been able to track our family history back to the sixteenth century thanks to church records...which presumably suggests that whatever my parents were offered the option of converting forcibly to Christianity or getting expelled...who knows..."

Their dialog drifted effortlessly as they chatted and joked in between bites of food and glasses of wine. They were each given a glass of "Jerez Dulce" sherry after their dessert, which Catherine defined as "delectably strong and nice." They wanted to stroll back to their flats because the weather was good, and none of them was ready to call it a night.

They headed out, taking their time and carrying on their conversation. Nora was a sweet and lively girl who made Catherine laugh, something she desperately required. As Nora talked of her hands being frozen, Catherine ignored her and clasped her hand in hers. Nora's expression of adoration was precious.

The age-old quandary arose in Catherine's mind when they entered Nora's apartment. What do I do now? Should I say goodbye to her? Do I hug her? What if she invites me inside?

"So, Catherine...

I had a great time with you today...

Would you like to come in...just for a moment?"

Oh my God, what do I do...what should I do...

Do I take the first date inside? What if...what if this continues... What pantyhose am I wearing this time? Do nice girls do so on their first date? Oh well, screw it...

"Sure, Nora, that will be lovely!"

Nora stayed in a two-story all-girls apartment with seven spaces and communal dining rooms, kitchens, and toilets. Her space was on the first level, with a view of a wide park.

"I'm sorry this place is such a shambles...you know...seven there's of us...hard it's to keep track of things...ahhh...and here's my castle, my home away from home," Nora said as she opened the door to her space. "Do you like anything to drink? Is it possible for me to bring you something? If you like, I have some Sangria downstairs in the fridge..."

"It will be fantastic, thank you."

"Here, sit on this while I get our glasses," Nora said, patting the cover of her bunk. Catherine could sense her as she slid down the stairs and then ran back up. "Here...they...are," she exclaimed, keeping two bottles and a frozen jug of Sangria. "I made that myself," she said as she poured wine into their bottles.

"Oh? Were you anticipating visitors?" Catherine teased with a playful remark.

"No...I mean...yes...no...not that's the case. I made it for my flatmates once, and they loved it so much that we now have a jug in the fridge at all times...we all chip in for the supplies, and everyone can have a glass."

"Oh...but who cares if they notice the pitcher is missing?"

"Nobody is staying the night. It's a Saturday, and everybody is gone, so we have the house to ourselves."

"Well, then, cheers...bottoms up!"

Nora sent her friend a crooked smile and almost shot Catherine with Sangria from her lips. She burst out laughing as she gasped for breath, falling into her bed in the process.

"What are you talking about? What's the big deal?"

"...haha...well...I just imagined something...it..." that's

"What are you talking about? Tell me...come on...tell me..."

Nora smiled sheepishly, a girlish look on her lips. "Well, when you said bottoms up, that's what I imagined..."

"What did you photograph?"

"I'm afraid I can't tell you..."

"What if I did...this?" Catherine said as she plunged her hands mercilessly into Nora's flanks, tickling her mercilessly. Nora writhed and screamed hysterically as Catherine ran her hands around her friend's naked body. She was ecstatic, delighted, and enthusiastic. Their tickling session quickly turned into a fun grappling match, which concluded with Catherine straddling Nora's chest and pinning her hands together with hers.

Their breathing was also labored as a result of their exertion. Catherine's hair had dropped in front of her, forming a veil between her and Nora's faces. Their smiles vanished as the gulf between them shrank. Nora's eyelids drooped and her lips parted; Catherine slid her elbows onto the bed and gingerly cupped her cheek between her hands. Their lips came together quietly, kindly, yet magically. Catherine remained motionless, goosebumps coursing across her body and a million butterflies fluttering in the pit of her stomach.

Catherine stroked Nora's cheeks as their tongues brushed softly, each of them savoring the sublime and mystical uniqueness of their first kiss. Nora raised her arms and put them around Catherine's back, squeezing their bodies close. Their kiss became more intense, and Catherine prodded her tongue out, hoping to match it with Nora's. Lips separated, and tongues swayed back and forth playfully while they both began hissing through their noses, neither trying to break the spell.

And there were other areas to investigate; Catherine turned her focus to her lover's neck, licking an earlobe and sending her extraordinarily agile tongue to investigate the inner folds. Nora exhaled forcefully with each twitch of her tongue through her delicate contact. She shifted her focus to her throat, gently biting and kissing along the way, ever the adventurer.

As she put her leg between Nora's legs, she felt the girl rub her groin on her. She could sense the fire and desperation in her movements. Catherine was not unaffected; she could feel her pussy lips engorged and rubbing into her pantyhose and pants. She was developing a lot of lubricants and could still sense the dampness of her pussy. Her nipples were painfully hard, grinding against the lining of her bra with each movement. But most importantly, she could feel the heat; her body was literally on fire from all the excitement.

Then clothes began to move everywhere, with a desperation Catherine had never felt before. She wanted to rub her tongue all over Nora's body, licking her pussy dry like a thirsty individual craves water in the desert. They were left with just their panties after frantic pulling and tugging at the offending clothes.

Nora had selected powder blue cotton pants and a white top, practically matching her hoodie and earrings to her underwear. Catherine opted for a more traditional, all-weather black. When they kissed again, Catherine unclasped Nora's bra while feeling nimble fingers undo hers. Catherine then lightly moved her beloved onto the bunk, feasting her attention on the beautiful body underneath her.

She took a moment to enjoy her breasts. Catherine loved their appearance, their perfectly upright posture, and their height, which she estimated to be a 32C with wide, almond-colored areolas and large, protruding nipples. Nora's nipples were slightly erect from their earlier kissing, and her areolas had bulged and widened slightly.

She softly put her right nipple inside her mouth after running her hands over them. She could see the nipple harden and expand as she swung her tongue around. Nora let out a light sigh of satisfaction. Her hands caressed Catherine's fur. She started to suckle on her breast, cupping it in her hand for greater leverage and sometimes offering her a slight bite. She switched sides, focusing her attention on the left nipple as her free hand played with the now gleaming right breast. As her tongue alternated between those glorious mounds, Nora let out soft moans of approval.

Catherine then did something unusual: she turned Nora over and let her lie on her tummy. Her hands began to move over her back, sending shivers down her lover's spine. She gradually shifted her focus to her lower back, her hands gliding across velvety smooth skin. Catherine's palms teasingly massaged her buttocks' globular delightfulness, creating repetitive motions on each cleft.

Nora murmured and purred like a cat while involuntarily opening her legs wider, allowing Catherine access to her inner thighs. She ignored it and continued stroking those wonderful legs down to her shock-clad bottom. She knelt slightly and hooked her thumbs on the waistband of her thong, gently peeling it off.

Catherine laid her fingertips tenderly on Nora's inner thighs, prompting her to whimper in agreement. Kneeling farther down, she could see inner lips protruding over lushly wrapped outer lips, as well as a thin strand of silvery liquid trickling gently into the bed. She made tiny suckling gestures with her tongue on the girl's buttocks. Nora replied by raising her buttocks slightly in the air.

Catherine traced her tongue all across the bare ass clefts, allowing tantalizing forays within the crack of her buttocks. Nora's face had broken out in goosebumps, and her soft purrs of delight had become more frequent. Catherine softly raised

Nora's breathtaking butt, exposing her dripping cunt in front of her eyes, by placing her palm under her stomach.

The sight was breathtaking. Nora's majestic roundness was on display with all its splendor. The girl has those severe killer curves and no flab on them. Catherine took a short pause before sending her tongue downwards into Nora's outer lips, which were now wet with her juices. She created circular movements with her lips, savoring the delicious flavor of her cunt and inhaling her intoxicating fragrance, hardly reaching her.

She rolled over gingerly, her back still lying on the bed. Her tongue drifted north once more, looking for other places that needed her help. With a sigh, Catherine put her lips on Nora's right breast, gently kissing the nipple. Nora could feel the tongue licking across the areola, a teasing combination of kisses, sucking, and chewing that made her writhe in pain and desire. Catherine sucked on the nipple until it was tough and popped out of her mouth. She moved her attentions to her left breast, not wanting to leave it unsatisfied, while her fingertips wickedly pinched the other already erect nipple.

Nora began tugging at Catherine's hair frantically, attempting to nudge her into her throbbing cunt as Catherine was sucking on her breast. This fueled Catherine's appetite even more; she tried to lick Nora's body clean before the girl virtually begged her to refrain.

Her lips moved down Nora's belly, licking and sucking her tummy after making sure she'd left behind her two very erect nipples. Moving down her stomach, she could fill her nostrils with her perfume once more. Catherine inhaled deeply as she rested her nose on Nora's pitch black pubic hair. The poor girl underneath her was now writhing and thrashing about as though she had a terrible rash on her back.

Catherine realized she'd punished both her boyfriend and herself sufficiently. She parted two very puffy and protruding inner lips with the tip of her tongue to expose the sopping entrance of Nora's vagina. She slid her snakelike tongue into the origins of her nectar, savoring the delicious flavor and sublime tightness of the surroundings. Her hesitant probes were quickly followed by determined thrusting.

Catherine was employing every trick in the book; one thumb circled Nora's protruding clit with cruel laziness. Another digit had made its way through her lover's puckered hole, softly massaging the delicate folded skin there.

Nora had been reduced to an incoherent rag doll at her hands by this stage. Her body was flailing about frantically as she attempted in vain to stuff some of her cunt inside Catherine's mouth. Her hands were frantically pulling at Catherine's hair, attempting to guide her tongue into her throbbing clit. She wasn't still, mumbling incoherently in both English and Spanish.

Nora drew in her breath, her body stiffened like oak, and her mouth let out a quiet scream. Catherine watched the walls of Nora's vagina contract rhythmically as she rode the surge of her orgasm. Catherine changed her mouth angle, her lips clamping closely on her throbbing clit, just as it seemed she had crested the swell.

This time, her scream was genuine. "Ay...ay...ay...Dios mios...ayyyy...maaaasss...massssssssssssssssssssssssssssssssss sssssssssssssssssssssssssssssssssssssssss Nora pushed her pelvis upward with intensity, and her body rocked dramatically with tremors while her hands desperately jammed Catherine's head into her vagina.

And, following a magnificent second stroke, it was all over. She slumped on her bunk, eyes closed and fully exhausted. There were a few cramps here and there as the aftershocks of her orgasms pierced her altered perception of truth.

"Aye ayeayeayeayeaye a

Madre de Dios, chica...you are simply fantastic..."

"I hope you had as much fun as I did."

"Enjoy doesn't even come close to describing it." Nora drew Catherine down beside her and nuzzled her ear. "It feels so good...so cozy in your embrace."

They cuddled like that before Catherine saw Nora's eyelids drooping. She began to rise, smiling, to dress. "Can you tell me where you're going?" She overheard Nora tell with a pouty tone.

"Back to my apartment. I've depleted you."

"It is not correct. I just need a moment to myself before it's your turn."

"I believe I can quit. Tomorrow, I need to get an early rise. There's a lot of research to do."

"Noooooo...could you please stay...please? Do you want to spend the night?"

Nora was kneeling on her bed, her hands almost in meditation, her swollen breasts hanging in front of Catherine's eyes. Her lips licked involuntarily as a result of the image. Nora was taken aback and couldn't help but smile. "Could you please? What about me? They'll feel sad if you're not around to caress them. "She said this as she began to play with her breasts.

Any determination Catherine may have had vanished quickly. "You made convincing points. In truth, there are two of them. I'll continue if three conditions are met."

Nora gave her a puppy grin. "All right...and these are?"

"One, I'll have to quit early tomorrow morning. I just need to get back on track with my studies. Two, you must allow me to use the wall side of your room. I toss and move too often that I could wind up on the floor if I didn't. Three...you'll have to make me kiss you at least twice more..."

"You've got a deal...except...three...obviously it's your turn to be on the receiving end..."

"Nuh-Uh...I have to kiss you again, or there's no contract."

"Awwwww...fine...but you're a tough bargainer..."

Nora drew her down for another steamy embrace as her hands were busy tugging at Catherine's black pantyhose. Yes, despite all their prior efforts, it was the only dress that remained on her. Catherine complied, and a rather sodden thong was quickly out of their path. A deft pair of nimble fingertips quickly made their way past her dark brown thatch and upwards, cracking her lips in the process. Catherine moaned in Nora's mouth; she'd had enough of being turned on. Her climax was right there with her. She began humping those wonderful digits in earnest without breaking their kiss.

Nora soon realized what was going on and snatched Catherine's a$$ with one hand as the other resumed its ministrations. Catherine was bucking her pelvis in a frenzy; she was close, really close, and Nora's tongue was plunged aggressively into her mouth just added to her arousal.

Her orgasm struck her like a bolt of lightning, a huge eruption emanating from her clitoris that exploded in waves across her body. The rhythmic contractions of her pussy walls extended across her body, giving the impression that her whole body was one huge pulsating mass. Nora had slowed down and avoided overt touch with the edge of her clit, but Catherine couldn't get enough of it. "No, don't you fucking stop...go on...yes...like that...yes...fuck...oh fuck...another one..."
Catherine let out a shriek-like hiss and began trembling violently. What began as a flash orgasm had exploded into two distinct ones that had effectively fused. Although the first was

aggressive, the second went on before Catherine feared she would pass out from all the stars and explosions she saw.

She eventually descended from her euphoria. As she opened her eyes, she noticed Nora clutching her juice-covered hand under her nose. She could sense a stream of blood running down her legs. When she glanced down, she was horrified to see a damp spot on the bedsheet.

"Shit...Did I just do all of this?"

"Nuh-uh...sure...all it's yours. What a shame to squander all of this...delicious...tasty...juice, "Nora punctuated each term for effect as she licked her cream-coated fingers clean. "By the way, you taste fantastic... I will eat this every day and not need to eat much else."

In Catherine's view, a lightbulb went off. "I'm feeling sticky and humid. Do you want to take a shower before we go to bed?"

"Sure...it shouldn't be that hard...

The shared bathtub is right next to us on our floor. Allow me to get a couple of towels and some shampoo."

Nora opened her room door and peeked, wrapping the towels around them; the coast was clear, and no sound could be seen. They tiptoed out of the room and into the shower, giggling. The green-tiled space was an old-fashioned white porcelain bathtub with different hot and cold water faucets, as is customary in the United Kingdom. However, several more recent additions, such as a shower curtain and a wall-mounted showerhead with a single handle water tap.

Nora knelt to switch on their tub, and Catherine couldn't help but notice the girl's sculpted a$$. Two perfect spheres of pure, unadulterated perfection that jiggled tantalizingly with her every step. Catherine could see Nora's puckered hole and the lushly covered lips of her vagina behind it with a hungry look. The girl's hair was already mated and glistening from their last lovemaking, and her lips were parted and slightly swollen, a clear indication that she was still turned on and eager for more.

Catherine couldn't help herself; she slipped a hand through the enticing void. Nora exclaimed and pressed her groin into Catherine's hand as she traced her fingertips between her lips' folds. "Fuck, that sounds amazing," Nora hissed. "Put...put a finger inside...fuck me..." Catherine couldn't help but comply. She slipped one and then two fingers into her, and they slid in so easily that the kid was virtually leaking the material again. Her other hand curled around her thigh, discovered her clit, and began flicking it around.

Nora's speech is incoherent once more. She was the sexiest thing Catherine has ever seen, with her head bent over the bathtub and raven hair falling all over her chest. Her thigh biceps bulged as she rose on her toes, ramming her cunt into Catherine's fingertips. Their fucking was anything but timid this time; Nora had gone too far and became very vocal.

Catherine did all she could to help her; she inserted a third finger and folded the four fingers in a bill-like formation. Nora didn't skip a beat; in reality, her pace increased. Who might have guessed that the shy, petite girl who confronted her the other day would turn out to be such a sex wolverine?

Nora's shriek jolted her out of her reverie. The raven-haired girl stormed in angrily and loudly. Whether there was someone in the nearby flats, they had undoubtedly heard them. Catherine kept rubbing the girl's clit until she was fully exhausted. Nora yelled, "Stop!" hoarsely. "No...no...no...no...no...no...no...no...no...no...no...no...no...no...no...no...no...no...no

Catherine grinned quietly to herself. The girl seemed to have been royally screwed, and there was a good possibility she'd be a teeny-weeny bit sore in the morning. Catherine thought to herself, "I know, Jesus." Four fingers went in there! Sure, the field is stretchy and has the potential to extend, but the girl had taken it in stride. She pressed her fingertips to her nose and closed her eyes. Delicious! The girl smelled and ate fantastically.

Meanwhile, Nora had leaned over the bathtub's edge, her head drooping into the steaming shower of water. Her legs were hanging over the tiled floor, and her butt was suspended in midair. Her lips were stretched open; her inner lips and the entrance to her vagina were reddish, evidence of the savagery that had occurred earlier.

"Come on, sweetie; you can do it. You'd like to take your shower standing up right now... It'll be beneficial to you."

"God, my God, God, God, God, God, God, God, God, That was completely nuts! That's something I've never done before. My muscles are aching...el cono...on its fire!"

"What's the deal with El Cono? So, let's go inside, and maybe I'll offer it a relaxing little kiss."

They both stepped into the bathtub and stayed behind the shower nozzle. After all those orgasms, the warm water felt calming and relaxing. Much better were the slipping, soap-covered hands caressing wet flesh. Those roving hands re-ignited the embers in no time. Nora sat cross-legged, her face level with Catherine's pubic hair, with a mischievous smile on her face. Catherine raised one of her legs and let it stand on the bathtub's lip, sensing Nora's purpose. Nora swooped in, her lips latched around Catherine's protruding clit.

Oh my God, this looks divine, thought Catherine. Then she felt hands snaking up her thighs, one palming her butt, the other poking inside her openings. Two of them went up to her vagina while another peered through her back fence. Catherine was melting from the sun, and the warm water spraying from the showerhead had little to do about it.

It was an extremely erotic setting; Catherine's eyes were closed, and all that could be heard were Nora's fingertips sloshing, dripping water, and gentle sighs leaving her lips. Nora sucked hard on her clit, causing an irritating suction effect. As if that wasn't enough, her tongue twirled around Catherine's button, causing her to tremble with delight. But it was the rhythmical pumping of the girl's fingertips that got to her. Catherine wasn't a big fan of anal pleasure; in truth, this was just the second time it had gone up there. But the triple hit on her crotch sent her overboard this time.

Catherine arrived, and her orgasm struck her hard and quick. This was no friendly wave of pleasure; it was a rogue wave that came out of nowhere and spun her about like a twig in a storm. She started her descent as rapidly as she had crested the wave...literally. Her knees buckled, and she might have fallen if Nora hadn't intervened with her steadying fingertips. She was completely exhausted; her belly was heaving, frantically struggling to fill her lungs with oxygen, and her pulse had gone haywire. When she opened her eyes, she noticed Nora's face with a crooked grin; the little devil had loved it and was laughing at her expense.

"You know I'll get you for that..."

"Not until I have you first!"

"I was supposed to feed you two more days, but you turned the tables on me."

"I'm already here...I haven't left!"

"God, you're a voracious eater, baby! Are you getting a sense of it yet?"

"Yeah, I think we can get some rest. What do you mean? Isn't it true that I'm a year younger than you? Should be considerate of the wishes of the elderly. I apologize for being so harsh on you, Catherine."

"How come you..."

Catherine turned the shower head toward Nora and flipped on the cool tap. Nora squealed as the cool water splashed across her breasts. There was a good old-fashioned splashing race, with plenty of laughing and amusing banter traded. Finally, the water became too cold for them, and they wanted to leave. And it couldn't have come at a better time when they heard sounds downstairs. They made a giggling run for Nora's bed, wrapping their towels around them. As the two girls snuggled into each other's embrace, a peaceful and blissful sleep enveloped them.

Vanessa

Vanessa posed nude in front of her closet mirror, her hair covered in a towel. She was debating whether to carry for her night out. Vanessa has spent a considerable amount of time in the bathroom smoothing her legs and armpits. Her pubic hair had been removed earlier in the day with a trip to the waxing salon. The agony had been unbearable, so she had stripped naked. Tonight, Vanessa was on a mission: she needed a rough, no-strings-attached fuck to get Catherine out of her mind.

Catherine has most likely entered her mind due to her series of bad boyfriends and lack of sex. Plus, they'd been best buds for years, and her mind was playing tricks on her. What she wanted was a huge night out paired with a random shag, she reasoned. She could still feel anxious, a mix of nervousness and horniness coursing through her veins. One-night stands weren't normally her thing; she avoided them, and you never know who you'd wind up in bed with. So she now couldn't care less. She figured she wanted a huge fat cock in her snatch.

She dressed in this frame of mind. This was a euphemism for what she had selected. Her clothing had been chosen solely for not getting in the way. Her pants were a crotchless thong, with two cords of lace lying on her outer lips instead of the normal triangle of silk on which her pussy lay. She was going commando; the thing didn't even have to be moved to the side to fuck.

Then she put on her thigh-high stockings; yeah, it was chilly, but pantyhose would just get in the way. She was going to rock a one-piece black strapless dress with a bodice instead of a bra. It stood just below her stockings and had soft folds underneath her waist, rendering it very simple to raise without taking it off. The top gave her the appearance of a serving wench, but that was the whole point of the ensemble. She'd accessorize with a black bolero jacket and stiletto, knee-high black leather boots. When it came to fast fucks, high heels were still a good idea because they raised her butt compared to the guy's junk.

She was only finishing up the rest of her mascara on her eyes when her intercom buzzed; her lab buddies had returned with the bus. It was time to roll because she was smoking.

"Hello there, lady! You look fantastic tonight, "Felicia, a tall hulk of a woman with an incredible collection of arms, chirped. Felicia dressed and posed like a kid in the lab. Tonight, though, she looked very pretty, if a little on the butch side, with her hair done up, make-up on, and a proper shirt, Vanessa concluded.

And there was Roberta, or Robbie as she was affectionately known. She had red hair and milky white eyes, and she had elven beauty. She normally wore jeans and black-framed frames in the lab, but tonight she wore a short denim skirt and a black velvet tee on top; her legs looked fantastic. Also, the lenses were no longer there, having been replaced by contacts. Her hair was styled in a shaggy pixie cut that perfectly framed her elegant features.

Elena, a Czech girl with model proportions, was the last but not least. Vanessa thought she was the most beautiful of them all. In the lab, she was still well-dressed, and her palms, considering the rubber gloves they had to wear on and off all the time, were still perfectly manicured. Tonight, she kept her sandy blonde hair in pigtails, and the black leather leggings she wore accentuated her long legs. Elena was still getting looks and wolf whistles on the street; in the lab, the men didn't dare to do that, so they settled for undressing her with their eyes. She didn't seem to mind or worry, however. The girl exuded an air of invincibility, and it was obvious.

Vanessa questioned why she had given so much attention to the other girls' clothing when they bantered back and forth while waiting for their taxi to drive them to their destination. Then her imagination played a trick on her, and she began to imagine how each girl might appear undressed. "No, no, no, no, no, no, no, no, no, no, no, no, I decline to participate in this game, "She pondered. She clenched her eyes shut as though doing that would rid her head of the distracting thoughts.

"Are you okay, Vanessa? You are a little pale."

"I'm good...just a spasm or something...I'll be fine..."

"Are you certain?"

"Sure, I'm great, boys...

I'm really on top of it."

They were on their way to the Tiger-Tiger, a posh three-story restaurant-club-bar in Manchester's Printworks district. The dress code was rather tight, and if the bouncers thought you weren't up to standards or your conduct was rowdy, you might quickly be kicked out. But they were four well-dressed, attractive young ladies, so that shouldn't be a challenge. In reality, when Vanessa asked if they could skip the line, the bouncer smiled happily and guided them inside.

They went to the second level, where there was a labyrinth of bars and dance floors. Vanessa bought a bottle of Bacardi rum and the regular mixers for them after they had settled into their stand. After that, they reserved a pitcher of tequila sunrise, which was accompanied by tequila slammers in shot glasses. Vanessa's mind was hazy still, but she was having a nice time, smiling and flirting with others.

There was this muscular jock-type man in a skin-tight black shirt milling around on the stand next to theirs. Normally, muscular muscle men weren't her thing, but she was wasted, horny, and the man reminded her of Tom Hardy in Warrior. They had been exchanging looks all night, and as the majority of her mates went off to a party, he approached her.

"Why are you alone tonight, such a lovely creature?"

"I'm not alone...I came here with my buddies," Vanessa laughed, blinking her eyelids at him, more intoxicated than she realized.

"Would you like to dance?"

"All right!"

They danced provocatively together, Vanessa grounding her already leaking crotch on his muscled leg as he groped her buttocks very aggressively. They embraced, and Vanessa felt one of his hands grabbing her neck and the other going beneath her shirt. Strong and heavyset digits made their way inside her vagina and shoved them deeply. It felt nice, but being touched anywhere else would have been much better, Vanessa reasoned. The kissing was a little sloppy, but his hug was sweet and solid, which felt amazing.

"I want to fuck you," he hissed into her ear, chewing her earlobe as he did so. "Here?" she inquired, a little dizzy. "Let's head to the men's room." They dragged her hand through the labyrinth of dark corridors and barged through a door. The white surgical light nearly blurred Vanessa's eyes as they struggled to adapt. In a barren cubicle, Tom, as she had labeled him in her head, half pulled, half thrust her. He created a semi-erect uncircumcised cock by unzipping his trousers. He pushed her to her knees with his hands. "Get it clean and wet for me," he ordered sternly.

Vanessa complied, tentatively taking the purplish head in her lips. Tom caught her hair with one fist and rammed his hardening shaft into her throat with the other. Vanessa stifled a sob. "Wait a minute...not that soon..." "Shut up, bitch...suck it up like the sweet little whore you are, and if you're lucky enough, I'll fuck you."

While the bobbing of her head, coupled with her alcohol poisoning, made her vision fuzzy, she eventually adjusted to his overzealous ramming.

"Get on your feet! Put your hands on the wall!"

"Shouldn't we use a condom? Outside, there's a condom dispenser..."

"Don't be concerned. I'm no longer dirty!"

"But...I'm not...I'm not...I'm not...I'm not...I'm not...I'm not...I'm not...I

He jammed her upper body against the upper toilet and stretched her legs instead of responding. When her head hung over the toilet tank, Vanessa watched it spin out of orbit. She felt his rough shaft slam through her insides without notice.

"Owww," she exclaimed dramatically. "Shut up, slut. Do you want us busted?" He put his hand over her lips, essentially muffling her up, without waiting for a response.

Vanessa's focus began to fade. Tears streamed from her eyes. Tom was now fucking her painfully. Her brain was throbbing with pain, and her stomach lurched as he pushed her back and forth. Tom arrived with a deep grunt; she could sense his semen as shot after shot of his spunk plastered the walls of her vagina. With a big plopping motion, he retreated almost as quickly as he had entered her. "You were a fine little whore back then," he sneered. He slammed the cubicle door shut behind him after zipping up his trousers.

Vanessa stood there, sticky liquid trickling down her thighs from her vagina. That's when the panic attack struck. He had infiltrated her! Her stomach began to heave as she hyperventilated. Her stomach retched, and vomit splattered from her mouth onto the toilet tank. When she slipped, her legs buckled, and her face almost collided with the toilet. She had little option but to flee! She wanted to support! She needed the services of a pharmacy!

Once her stomach had done emptying its contents, she was able to stay erect with great difficulty. She propped her body in front of the drain, half staggering, half lurching. When she glanced in the mirror, she felt she saw a ghost; her hair was unkempt, her make-up was all over her face, and her complexion was a ghostly white. She rinsed her mouth as best she could and cleaned her cunt and thighs with hand towels to remove the disgusting material. At the time, she looked as though she wanted to die. She had never felt so ashamed and exploited in her life, and it was all her fault, she reasoned.

Another panic disorder struck her as her mind began to assess her situation. He could have HIV, he could have all kinds of STDs, I could be pregnant, she said, and her stomach retched once more. She managed to steel her nerves after round two of vomiting was over; she was solid, and she had to get through this. She had little choice but to abandon and take things into her own hands.

After cleaning herself up to the best of her ability, she went out to meet her friends to inform them that she was going. Her motor abilities were all over the place, but she managed to zig-zag back to their stand. She picked up her bag and texted her friends that she wasn't feeling good and that she was going early. In retrospect, it was much easier for her to stop them than to humiliate herself in front of her friends. "What do I do now? I have a medical emergency and must head to the hospital. I need assistance...Catherine..."

Catherine

The chirping of a bird hit Catherine's ears, and she laughed. She had a wonderful dream in which she was sitting under a massive apple tree with Nora, all nude and biting at the same apple. Droplets of apple juice trickled down their chins as they bit into the apple, which was light red and juicy. They'd laugh and kiss each other until they were clean. But...wait a minute...what was this damned bird doing chirping so loudly? That wasn't a duck; it was her cellphone. She opened her eyes and looked at Nora's mechanical clock. The time was 02:35, and the numbers were tall, red, and shiny. Who the hell will call her at such an inopportune hour? "Make it off, Catherineaaaa," Nora whined. "Hold on...need to double-check...maybe it's the people from home, they never have the time zones correct."

When she looked at the screen, she noticed Vanessa's familiar face flashing. "Yes?" she rasped, her voice hoarse. "Is that you, Catherine? Is it you, sir? "With shaky expression, she overheard her friend tell. Something was wrong, as flashing lights went off in her head. She stood up on the bunk, quietly beckoning Nora to "shush." On the other end of the phone, she could hear sobbing. "Greetings, Vanessa! Where have you gone? What transpired?"

"I...I require your assistance...I..." The sentence was incomplete. Fresh bursts of weeping and heaving disrupted Vanessa's voice. Catherine watched in disgust as her companion puked out her blood.

"Vanessa," she almost yelled now. "Calm down; I need to know where you are so I can come to get you."

"I...I'm on my way to the University Hospital...I...I was abused..."

Catherine's mind raced with horror and agony as she remembered what she had just experienced. "Oh my goodness! No way! That's awful. Wait a minute; I'll be right over. The road are you on?"

"I believe I'm on Upper Brook's sidewalk...the hospital's sidewalk..."

"Just...just hold tight, I'm on my way!"

Nora stared at her with skepticism. "What transpired?"

"My oldest friend had been raped. She's on her way to the doctor... I have to go look for her."

"Oh my goodness! That's worse."

"Yeah...I'm sorry to bother you like that, but I have to get on."

"Sure, sure, no problem. Let's go! I hope she's on fire. Just text me when you return to your apartment..."

"Will do," Catherine said, then shot off like an arrow with a chaste kiss on her lips. She was speeding through the empty streets, thanking her lucky stars now and then for wearing her trainers on her date. When she got to Upper Brook and Hathersage Lane's intersection, she slowed down and began frantically searching for her companion. She discovered her a little later, collapsed against a lamppost, dry-heaving; her stomach had long since drained its contents.

Catherine was almost in tears as she saw her like that. She suppressed her shock and steeled her nerves by bringing her hands to her lips. She wanted to be strong for her mate, who needed her right now.

"There, Vanessa!"

"Catherine ...'s you? Thank you, God, "she said before collapsing on the icy pavement

"There, Vanessa!" Catherine leaned over her friend and picked her by her armpits. Her skin was cold to the touch, with an unnatural bluish hue. Her skin was soaked with vomit and dirt; she'd fallen over a lot of times while walking to the hospital.

Catherine reached into her bag for some wet wipes and began cleaning her friend up as best she could. Vanessa was weeping and sobbing, having finally collapsed now that Catherine was with her. Catherine spruced her up and forced her to sit up straight. She removed her hoodie and pulled it over her head; Vanessa was shivering uncontrollably, and Catherine was terrified that she might pass out. She'd have a serious challenge on her hands if it happened. She removed her boots after forcing the hoodie on Vanessa. Stiletto heeled boots were not going to support her in her drunken condition, and they were most definitely the cause her friend had fallen over too many times. It's better to step in her stockings than to trip her.

"Come on, Vanessa...one more push...the hospital isn't far...we just need to walk a little farther."

Vanessa remained uncomfortably on her feet, struggling with effort. "My brain...my head...it just feels fine when my head stoops down..."

"I know, sweetie...but you have to support me here...help me so I can help you. I'll be there with you every step of the way, but I can't drag you to the doctor on my own. We have to handle things one action at a time. I swear I'll be right there beside you."

Vanessa made it to the hospital's emergency department by gritting her teeth and relying heavily on Catherine's assistance. Paramedics hurried to her aid, placing her on a stretcher and covering her with a blanket. Catherine, who was standing at her side, told the head nurse about what had occurred.

It was a Saturday night, and the place was teeming with drunks and people who had been in traffic crashes. Catherine was stared at sympathetically by the lead nurse. "Keep an eye on her at all times; she'll need all the support she can offer. We can't assign her immediate preference since she isn't seriously ill. What I'll do is hook her up to an IV line and prescribe medication to her. At the very least, that could help her recover from her alcohol overdose. So she'll be sent in for a gynecological test, and if it reveals something, she'll either press charges by our in-hospital police department, or you should drive her home."

Catherine praised the nurse and stood next to Vanessa's stretcher, squeezing her side. When the time elapsed, Vanessa began to calm down, which resulted in yet more screaming fits.

"What did I do? What did I do? "She kept repeating herself. Catherine cradled her in her arms and attempted to console her the best she could, caressing her hair and whispering soothing phrases. Catherine cradled Vanessa's head in her lap as she checked out.

Two stretcher-bearers arrived at four a.m. and escorted Vanessa into an inspection area. Catherine was permitted inside at all hours, at the behest of the head nurse, clutching her friend's wrist. They expertly positioned her on a gynecological test table, where the gloved doctor was still waiting. Vanessa began shivering uncontrollably after they stripped her clothes and dressed her in a paper robe. "Is it you, Catherine? Is there all they ought to do? Is it required? "She said this as tears streamed down her cheeks once more.

The doctor, luckily a female doctor, took her hand in hers and looked sympathetically at her.

"It will just take a minute, sweetheart. I'll be patient with you. I want to see whether there are any skin gashes or other types of bruises or bleeding. It will assist us in your treatment. Simply grab your friend's hand, and I'll walk you through it. If you experience some discomfort, nausea, or fainting, lift your hand quickly, and I will stop. Okay, sweetheart?"

Vanessa gave a weak nod. She let her legs be put in the stirrups while clutching Catherine's hand for dear life.

"Okay, honey...with my gloved fingertips, I'm going to brush around your labia majora softly...

Are you happy to begin right now?"

The doctor examined the area for bruising, skin ripping, or blood. She then dilates her vaginal canal with a speculum and collects numerous tests from there. She patted Vanessa's thighs, and they were finished. She then examined her upper body for any wounds or damage and discovered none.

"Despite your misfortune, I have some positive news for you, darling. You have no scratches or fractures and no skin lesions. Your genitals are in excellent condition, except for a minor skin rash. This is fantastic news because it drastically decreases the risk of developing HIV."

Vanessa flinched noticeably at the vibration. "...now...I'm going to ask you a couple of questions, and you're going to have to tackle them the best you can. The more precise your responses, the greater your treatment..."

"All right..."

"First and foremost, do you want to file charges? If indeed, I'll have to do several additional tests on you, such as looking for nail scrapings, doing a toxicological blood exam to screen for drugs, and so on... What do you want?"

"All I want to do is go home and worry about this..."

"It's your decision, sweetie...off the record, I highly advise you to press charges, but it's entirely up to you. Now...I need to find out a couple more information... Can you recall whether he ever inseminated you?"

Vanessa's face turned flushed with humiliation. "Yes...he finished inside me...there was no condom used..."

"Yes, I had the same feeling. Seminal fluid traces can also be seen on the thighs. We've collected samples for multiple lab tests... Are you currently taking a birth control prescription?"

"No...no contraception..."

"All right...when did your last cycle begin?"

"Oh, twenty-one days ago..."

"How is the menstrual cycle?"

"Twenty-eight or twenty-nine days, with a five-day bleeding period..."

"Okay, odds are you've avoided the bullet of an unintended birth, but we're not taking any chances. I'll prescribe you tablets to chemically stimulate your cycle as soon as we're done. It'll sting a little, and you may bleed a little more than normal, but at least you'll be at peace... What are vaccinations now? Have you had your hepatitis vaccinations?"

"Yes, I've had type A and type B vaccinations...

I've even had the Gardasil HPV test."

"You're a good kid...

Now...I'm afraid I'll have to prescribe a slew of medications for you to carry. You will be sent blood tests shortly after we conclude here. We're looking at STIs and HIV. To protect the HIV situation, I'll now recommend five days of retroviral medications."

"Oh my God..." Vanessa began to shiver once more.

"This is performed solely as a precaution," the doctor quickly said. "You were lucky to be free of tears and bruises. As a result, the odds of developing HIV are smaller than 1%, but we're not taking any chances. Then I'll administer a combination of three antibiotics to treat Gonorrhea and Chlamydia. We'll have to wait for the analysis of the blood sample to determine the rest. You'll be great, sweetheart. Don't be concerned with it. Your friend here did an excellent job, "she said, nodding to Catherine. "Can we now let her go so she can get you a fresh batch of clothes while you wait for your blood samples?"

Vanessa agreed with a smile. Catherine rummaged through Vanessa's bag, found her key and card, and dashed for their dorm. After grabbing a pair of sweatpants, she ran back to the hospital, new underwear, sneakers, boots, and a scarf. It was now almost six o'clock in the morning, and the day's tension and pressure were beginning to take their toll. But she also had work to do; Vanessa needed to be returned to her flat and cared for.
Over at the facility, she assisted Catherine in getting ready, collected her things in a big bag, and took another, smaller bag with her prescription medications. They found their way back to Vanessa's flat, keeping her by the waist. Catherine assisted her in undressing, removing her shoes, and putting on her pajamas.
"Is it you, Catherine? Do you want to sleep with me? Will you please?"

"Of course, whatever you want, sweetheart. Want me to go get my pajamas, and I'll be right there with you in a flash."

She went to Vanessa's apartment and saw her sleeping. Catherine breathed a sigh of comfort as she texted Nora that all was well and crawled her body next to her friend's. She laid awake, thinking about the activities of the night. If she were up for it, she'd have to ask Vanessa for more information in the morning. However, what a night it had been...

Vanessa

A flickering glow illuminated Vanessa's eyes. She rubbed her eyes wide, bringing her hands to her face. When she looked back, she saw Catherine lying on her side, facing her. Her face lit up with a grin. She said to herself, "God, she was so gorgeous." But then that thinking triggered the activities of the previous night, and...had she peed herself? Peering under the sheets, she was horrified to see a red smear between her thighs. Her time wasn't expected for another week. Then the cogs of her head started turning, and she recalled the medication she took the night before, the so-called "next day tablet," among other things.

She frantically attempted to stand up to go to the bathroom, but her stumbling prompted Catherine to stir. Vanessa went into a panic; she couldn't let Catherine see her like that!

"Can you tell me what time it is?"

"I'm not sure...just need to go to the bathroom..."

Catherine noticed Vanessa hugging the quilt to her stomach as she raised one eye. "Are you okay?"

Vanessa could feel tears running down her face. "I...I...made an meeeeeeeeeeeeeeeeeeeeeeeeeeeeeeeeeeeeeeeeeeeeeeeeeeeeeeeee eeeeeeeeee

Catherine recognized the issue; in any other situation, they would have laughed it off, but in Vanessa's current condition, making comments about the Japanese flag would just make matters worse. She soothed and caressed her mate as though she were a mother cradling her infant before the sobbing ended. Then, taking her by the back, she led her to her en-suite bathroom and assisted her in undressing. While the bleeding was excessive, the doctor had forewarned her about it.

The steaming water felt amazing on Vanessa's skin and made her relax. She was very irritated with herself at the time. She was furious about the foolish gamble she had taken the night before. And she was upset that she was always crying; she had always been a calm and intelligent person, but now she was a quivering mess. As she opened the bathroom door, she was welcomed by a cheerful Catherine, who gave her the towel and sanitary pads. When she noticed the tampons, Vanessa flinched. Inserting something in there, for the time being, is probably not a brilliant idea.

While she dressed in the clean clothes that Catherine had carefully laid on her bunk, she was struck by how well Catherine had taken care of everything: the soiled laundry had been wrapped and put in a washing bassinette to soak. She had arranged her clothes and placed them on her bunk. She had removed the blood-stained bedsheets and dropped them in the laundry hamper before searching Vanessa's closet for sanitary pads and tampons.

Vanessa's eyes welled up with water again, except this time they were tears of thanks. "I...I...can't...thank you sufficiently..." sobbed Vanessa as Catherine kissed her tenderly in her hug.

"Don't worry, sweetheart; it will be well..."

"You're so precious, and I've been so cruel to youuuuuuuuuuuuuuuuuuuuuuuuuuuuuuuu

"Heeeeeeeeeeeeeeeeeeeeeeeeeeeeeeeeeeeeeeeeeeeeee
Listen...I'll tell you all... Why don't you put on your sneakers and join me for a quick walk? You know, have some fresh air and

maybe some pancakes if you're feeling adventurous. It'll be beneficial..."

"All right..."

They marched hand in hand, side by side. Vanessa found it very reassuring to feel the warmth of Catherine's hand permeate her own. Her presence was like a balsam, helping to cure her wounds and clearing up her mind.

"You know...after last night's antics, I owe you a huge apology and a clarification..."

"You don't owe me anything. You'd have done the same thing. That's why we have mates."

"No, but I have to get this off my chest..."

"You don't have to tell me anything if you don't want to. It's all pretty raw, I mean."

"No...I don't need to...anyway...the reason I didn't want to press charges was that, in part, I brought this on myself...for reasons I can't tell you Catherine...at least...not now..." Vanessa sighed and walked away. "We went out with the lab girls last night, you see, planning on getting a huge one and everything. I was itchy, if you know what I say, and on the lookout for a shag. I realize it was slutty of me, but I thought I wanted it at the time.

We drank a lot...and I mean A LOT. I recall each of us having one bottle of rum, a pair of pitchers, and some shots of tequila. As you would expect, I was completely broken and unable to think. Then this man approaches and asks for a dance; I'm well beyond tipsy, but he has no trouble hooking up with me. We ended up embracing and loving up in a hallway, and then...he took me in a men's room cubicle. He was rough, but I didn't mind at first because I was all into a little spice, or so I hoped.

When he pulled me to my knees and gagged me with his dick, the first alarm went off. The second red flag came when he declined to use a condom, even though I had suggested it, and there was one of those dispensers in the restroom. He then became angry and called me names...he shoved me against the wall and...well...did me from behind...it hurt, I think I wasn't properly lubricated... I couldn't stop myself because I was so out of it. I felt like puking because of the swaying motion. The bastard then finished inside, and that's when I got my first panic attack. I managed to crawl back to our stand after puking my heart out, most likely owing to the alcohol and utter fear about what had just happened. Since the girls were nowhere to be seen, I took my bag and exited.

I felt like I was short of air, and my stomach couldn't avoid heaving and retching, even if there were just bile and saliva coming out. My shoes were murdering me, and I was freezing. I fell many times along the way...and then I realized I desperately wanted assistance...and...and you were my guardian angel...you came for me... Thank you so much! I...I hope I didn't sabotage anything for you... You mentioned going on a date..."

"You didn't wreck everything, sweetie...we were just sleeping..."

Vanessa took Catherine's hand in hers and turned to face her. "You remind her that she can take good care of you. She's a very fortunate girl; there aren't many people in the universe who are as kind-hearted as you... I wish you the best of luck with her..."

"Whoa...don't get too far ahead of ourselves...yes, I like her...cool she's and friendly and...and...erm...the sex was sublime...and...I shouldn't be talking to you regarding sex after tonight..."

"No, no...keep going...

I'm just a big ear waiting to know all the gory facts. First and foremost, you're beautiful when you blush, and second, I'd like chapter and verse, "Vanessa said, completely forgetting her predicament and revealing a glimpse of her former self for the first time.

Catherine grinned and catered to her mate. That was it; they went back to being two peas in a pod, laughing and enjoying a fun time.

Winter of 2014

Catherine

On the rainy, gray February Saturday, Catherine awoke late. Her mood was melancholy, which reflected the weather. It was the first day of her winter break, her tests had ended the day before, and she was expected to be in a good mood. Nonetheless, she was depressed; she was also contemplating her breakup with Nora.

It had been too nice to be real, she reasoned. All had occurred at breakneck speed; their first embrace, first time, first "I love you," it had all happened so quickly. All was so fine. Nora was a new individual when they returned from their Christmas holiday. She seemed detached, as though she was seeking to hide her. Catherine had been perplexed at first, then wounded, and finally furious. Nora had bent her head and claimed they couldn't be together anymore until she eventually approached her in person. She hadn't come out to her parents, and when she informed them she was gay and with another child, they went crazy; they told her not to repeat that nonsense and to watch her move, or they'd kick her out of her graduate program.

Catherine had begged her, telling her that they should be discreet, that she'd finish in a semester and then look for work, but to no use. They'd split up amicably, but Catherine's heart had been broken. Fortunately, she had tests coming up, and the constant studying took her mind off her heartache. But now that she'd done, she could feel the emptiness and wounds in her bones. She reasoned that she ought to divert her attention elsewhere. Vanessa, were you awake? She'd more likely be back at her lab.

"Come on...pick it up, pick it up!"

"How are you?"

"Let's see...Vanessa? Hello, my name is Catherine..."

"Just a minute..." Catherine could sense the rubber gloves being removed. "...okay...my apologies. So, what's the deal? How did last night's party go?"

"I did not attend. It didn't feel right."

"What do you mean?"

"Listen, I was curious if we could get together...just for a few minutes...

I know you're super-busy, but I need to speak with you."

"Oh, double oh? What transpired? What have I overlooked? Did you make a mistake on a test or something? Since you shouldn't be too concerned about it, you can still compensate and..."
"It's not like the exams went well. I need to speak with you, just not over the internet. "Do you have some spare time today?"
"Hmmmmmm..."
I've just begun a twelve-hour loop...
Warming up the cells, feeding the cells, expanding the cells...the usual nonsense. But it's Saturday, and no one is here. You are welcome to come over and sign in as a guest. You'd hold me company, and we'd be able to chat. If you don't pass out from exhaustion, I'll buy you dinner after we're finished. So, what do you think?"
"I'll be there in twenty minutes." I'll call you and ask you to let me in."

Catherine put on her beloved black leggings, a dark pink hoodie, and matching shoes and began jogging towards the biology school. The cool weather felt refreshing on her skin, so she took a step forward. As she worked, she could see her ponytail jumping about. Her eyes began to well up. No way, goddamnit, she wasn't going to scream. She quickened her stride, her long legs virtually devouring the gap. She could feel them burning, but she didn't mind; the freezing breeze was shearing her lungs, but she enjoyed the discomfort. The feeling of speed was intense, electrifying, and exhilarating. She was liberated, and her mind was clear. She grinned and eased to a steady trot to catch her breath. It had looked simply fantastic.

She arrived at the biology building's spectacular glass door, sweaty and slightly out of breath. She sat in the lobby, waiting for Vanessa to arrive and sign her in. They were upstairs on the second landing, in Vanessa's mutual office, a short time later.

"So, what's the deal?" What are you doing here if you aren't drinking or loving your free week from this slavery? Not that I'm moaning about the company...but when I'm in between routines, I might cut my wrists with a spoon out of boredom."

"I ended my relationship with Nora."

"Can you repeat that, Houston?"

"You understood me correctly. We split up. It unfolded just after we returned from our Christmas vacations. Fortunately, I was knee-deep in homework, which held my mind busy, but today...I wanted someone to unload..."

"However, what happened?" Any time you mentioned her, you appeared overjoyed."

"I was pleased, and we were happy." But, come to think about it, I did have this nagging thought in the back of my mind. When I'd ask her about our joint ambitions, such as moving together, she'd be evasive and noncommittal. I didn't give it much consideration because I was head over heels in love at the time. Then, after she returned from Spain shortly after New Year's, she avoided me. When I got hold of her, she begged me to end our relationship. She had come from a religious family; she had not come out to her community, and this graduate program here in the UK had seemed like an opportunity for her to free herself. As she told her parents about us during the holidays, they had a fit and tried to kick her out of the program.

I'm not sure what they rammed through her brain, but no matter what I told her...I tried reasoning, pleading, begging...yes, I even got down on my knees...she wouldn't budge. We split into good terms, but if it hadn't been for the exam time, I would have gone into a deep depression. I suppose the fact that I didn't have time for it to sting me, though, spared my sanity.

"Oh no...and you held it all inside you for a month!"

"As I mentioned, it worked out for the better. I didn't want to come to you earlier because the worst-case scenario would have been for me to collapse. I couldn't manage it, but I took it on the chin and soldiered on. I'm not pretending it doesn't hurt...because it does...a ton... I never imagined myself saying, "I'm grateful for my exam time..."

"Oh, sweetheart...come on over...hug time!"

"Vanessa...no...no...no...no...no...n

"I'm not sure it's a smart idea..."

"I love you!"

Vanessa embraced and patted her friend on the shoulder. The first sob arrived, a slow, almost quiet sob filled with excruciating "whys." The dam then broke. Vanessa hugged her mate, sensing her discomfort, caressing her back, and saying softly, "It's okay." The weeping eventually stopped; the crying had cleansed her spirit, and she felt stronger for it.

"Thank you so much; I think I just wanted that..."

"At any moment, sweetheart, at any time...

Listen, I'll tell you what...if you stay for another couple of hours, I'll call it a day, and we'll head out for an early dinner. Then we should head to the cinema and enjoy a rom-com or whatever while eating ice cream. "What do you think?"

Catherine blew her nose and rubbed her eyes with a Kleenex. That had become so cathartic. She was doing much happier now, and Vanessa's proposal seemed to be encouraging. A night at the movies appeared to be just what she wanted.

Vanessa

They went to the Manchester Printworks multiplex after filling up at the Chinese buffet restaurant they picked for dinner. Vanessa let Catherine pick what they'd watch, and after some deliberation, they settled on Vampire Academy: They Suck at School. The advertisement poster seemed promising enough, and the "sucking at kindergarten" pun seemed amusing enough.

"Are you certain that this is what you want?" It's defined as an action/fantasy film."

"I'm sure of that. I need something that would be impossible to miss right now. I don't want to hear about it."

"All righty...let me get the tickets, and you pay for the Ben & Jerry's."

They arrived at their theater hall after buying their seats and the biggest bucket of ice cream that the seller had to sell. They had selected a multiplex with nice armchair seats that suited your back posture and armrests that could be elevated if desired.

They all sank in with ease. The film began, and both seemed to be fully immersed in the narrative. Vanessa, on the other hand, maintained steely looks at her mate. In the faint, flashing illumination of the theatre, her face shone and then darkened based on the scene. As she looked at Catherine, she noticed a pleasant feeling that she couldn't quite place, but it was a sweet and welcome feeling nonetheless.

After finishing their ice creams, they both rested their hands on the armrest, with Catherine's palm on top of hers. It seemed normal to Vanessa, much as it would if she were out with a man. Later, Catherine happily shocked her by removing the armrest and snuggling her chin on top of her shoulder. And that was the end of Vanessa's attention span; she couldn't focus on the movie they were having as though her life relied on it.

It dawned on her that she felt genuine affection and desire for Catherine, not spiritual, friend-like attachment. True, Catherine had been her best friend initially, but what she was feeling now clarified several problems and raised a whole new set of questions for her. Did she adore her as a pal? Yes, but she felt more than that in her bones. Their close kiss and the magnetism she had sensed when Catherine had momentarily been. The unparalleled horniness she had experienced while on her lesbian fact-finding trip. The fright she'd felt as Catherine jokingly whispered in her ear. The incredible and unexplained envy she had felt when Catherine discussed Nora for the first time. Her outright dumb action the next day, getting wasted and running after some random jerk-off. The attention to detail, the wardrobe of her friends, the reverence for Catherine's figure.

So, where did that leave her? Was she a lesbian? She didn't feel much better for herself until admitting it. She ought to hear more, but first, she wanted to feel the comfort of Catherine's cuddle. She smiled to herself as she kissed the top of Catherine's head, eliciting a puppy-like grin in response.

Finally, the credits rolled, and they had to find their way out.

"Thank you once more," Catherine said, her eyes shining with sincerity. "You've helped me feel so much stronger."

"No, it should be me who thanks you. I'd be spending a miserable Saturday in the lab if it weren't for you."

Catherine

What she expected to be a day of doom and gloom turned out to be quite the opposite. Catherine had cried on Vanessa's shoulder, and it had raised a tremendous weight off her chest. They shared a great time, much like the old days. And she'd feel so at ease cuddling her head in the nook of Vanessa's ear. In reality, unless she were completely wrong, she would bet money that Vanessa had enjoyed it as well. But it was a thought for another day; right now, she wanted to relax because she was exhausted.

They had returned to their hall of residence in complete quiet, in contrast to the constant chatting and banter that had occurred earlier in the day. Vanessa seemed to be lost in thought, which Catherine decided not to interrupt. She did capture her steely looks at her when she didn't think she was looking. Catherine considered it funny but chose to remain silent.

They kissed goodnight, and Catherine had turned her back on Vanessa, walking towards the door of her section, when she heard Vanessa's voice: "Catherine wait..."

She turned back to see Vanessa approaching her. "Wait up," she said once more. When Catherine arrived, she stared at her with suspicion, but Vanessa stayed silent. She had something she wanted to say but couldn't quite get out.

"I'm a little chilly. "Would you like to move in?"

"Catherine."

"Are you sure?"

"I have something important to tell you."

"Would you like to tell me inside?"

"No...you'll think this is ridiculous..."

"What if I covered my eyes and didn't peek?"

Vanessa smiled nervously. There was a long pause between them. As they exhaled, the white security lights highlighted the halos of their breaths. Vanessa locked her gaze on her and didn't let go of her.

"This may be the dumbest thing I've ever done..."

Vanessa took a step forward, almost staggering, then laid her palms on Catherine's cheeks. They stood with their faces inches apart and their breathing hard.

"Would you please love me?" Catherine's voice came out in a small whisper.

Instead of responding, Vanessa closed her eyes and leaned forward. Their lips allowed the tiniest of touch. They remained in that place, eyes closed, breathing heavily, lips slightly touching. It looked like a dream come true and a nightmare at the same time to Catherine. She felt secret tears well up in her eyes, but she didn't want to run, didn't dare to move.

She sensed Vanessa whisper in her mouth without breaking touch. "Anakin...uh...uh...uh...uh...uh...uh...uh...uh...uh...

As they both raised their doors, their faces were just a few centimeters apart. "Anakin...Catherine...Ummm...I'm not sure how to put this..." Vanessa said quietly. "I umm...I just loved cradling you in my arms in the movie theater...ummm...in...in...in...in a non-friendly way..."

Despite her tears, Catherine grinned. "That's a pretty long statement to tell you like me...in a not-so-friendly way."

Vanessa was uneasy and tongue-tied. Catherine snatched Vanessa's hand away from her cheek and clasped it between both of her own.

"Pay attention, Vanessa...

I sensed that as well, okay? There is something else about us than friendship. Believe me; there's nothing I'd rather do right now than kiss you and throw you on my bed. You haven't got a clue...

Vanessa's face flushed, and she lowered her head. "There's no simple way to put it, Vanessa... I'm madly in love with you. I'm completely, hopelessly, completely, madly in love with you. I've been in love with you since I knew what it meant to be in love. At first, I assumed it was a childish crush, something that would pass. Then, in high school, I was perplexed. Why was I feeling this way? What was it about girls that drew me in? What was it about my best friend that drew me in? What was it with boys that I didn't like? I assumed that it would go out as if it were a disease healed with drugs if I dated.

I observed you going out with the boys. I sat back and watched while you told me about your romantic adventures. I soaked it all in like a knife to the core. And I had to do so with a smile on my face because no one, particularly you, should know that I was into girls. I learned to deal with my unrequited love in the same way as one continues to live with a debilitating illness. I was hoping beyond hope that I'd meet someone else, another girl to love and spend my life with.

But you were still there...never far below the horizon, no matter how hard I tried to keep my feelings for you hidden. They'd go inactive for a bit, then resurface with a vengeance at the smallest provocation.

You mean...you say you liked our embrace? Will you have any idea how this affects me? "What does this do to me?"

Catherine could see Vanessa was crying now, so she wanted to say these words; she had to get them out of her system. She continued, squeezing her friend's hand firmly.

"Sweetie, trust me...seeing you weep hurts like you've inserted a barbed javelin through my core." As much as it hurts me to admit it, I don't want another game of hiding and seek. I don't want to be anyone's toy. I don't like it anymore. I don't want to be a spanking bank...

Now...I'm ready to love you unconditionally and wholeheartedly. But, Vanessa, I'm gay. I'm a dyke, a lesbian, and a carpet eater. It took me years to come out to myself—years of unbearable agony. I'm no longer afraid of who I am, and I'm no longer interested in running. That's in the past, and anybody who doesn't like it should leave.

I present you with my heart. But I'm a homosexual one. I'm looking for a full-fledged, public, and dedicated partnership. Were you willing to go along with it? Are you even able to consider what that could imply for you? Since I'm not doing the friendship thing, on the other. I'm not trying to be someone's female confidante.

Vanessa, I adore you. I love you...and even though you've always been with me, I've always been single... So you're going to do that because I love you. You'll walk away and reflect. Consider everything I've placed on your tray. You should take as much time as you want. In the meantime, we won't see each other...no phone calls, messages, or e-mails... Come back after you've answered the questions I've set out for you..."

Vanessa was sobbing freely now, but she agreed in support. "Can I...can I only have one more kiss?"

They embraced and held in tears, not able to let go of the other. Catherine finally moved her away softly. It was finally time... Vanessa dried her tears, twisted, and walked forward.

"Just please...please come back fast," Catherine said when her knees gave out, and she slid with her back against the stone. She screamed, clutching her knees until she ran out of tissues. She went into her home, exhausted, and fell on her bed, clothes and everything, sleeping the sleep of the dead.

Vanessa

She dashed back to her bed, where she felt as though she were suffocating. She could remember the agony Catherine felt. She could see that this discomfort was all too true. She had little choice but to act. She wanted answers now, and she needed them quickly. Crying and feeling sorry for herself wasn't going to get her anywhere. Catherine had assigned her a task: either deliver or drown.

She booted up her laptop and began searching the internet for answers. Reading on what it was like to be homosexual and seeing stories of actual women talking about their encounters. She began to see details that had previously gone unnoticed. How she had always felt Catherine was lovely and how she had always wanted to satisfy her. How she'd mostly looked at other attractive women, searching them out and admiring their appearance. How her sex life with men was a disaster, and how she'd deluded herself into thinking it was simply the way she was wired. She'd rarely experienced orgasms with her former lovers, how she'd lied to make them proud, how she had drowned herself in work to hold her mind busy.

To her shock, she realized she had gone to England not because her parents forced her to but because she needed to get away from Catherine. Maybe it hadn't been a deliberate idea, but it was now crystal clear to her. She had fled. She had not only imposed suffering and meaningless marriages on herself, but she had also caused her best friend untold agony. In her support, she said that she hadn't heard and couldn't have known. Had she attempted to find out? Or she? Or had she simply fled?

What would it be like to be with a girl? She'd have to tell her parents, of course. She'd have to "come forward," which was often said. She'd have to go back to Canada with that; there was no chance she'd do it over the internet or Skype. What for her pals? Her nearest associates will be told directly. The remainder will be strictly on a need-to-know basis. Would she miss any of her friends? Perhaps, but if they were lost for such a cause, they didn't qualify to be on her friend list in the first place.

So, how about her parents? It was going to be difficult. Her parents were traditional, and she was the only child. They had high hopes for her. She adored them, but she refused to allow them to influence her judgment. She was a mature lady, extremely competent in her field of research, and self-sufficient. She wished they'd recognize and support her for who she was. There would be suffering if this did not happen. She was in a lot of agonies so that she couldn't get away from it. All had to face the beat, including her.

As a result, when she thought about it, it was never a matter of whether she wished to be with Catherine or not. She'd desired that all along but hadn't dared to admit that to herself. It was still there in the back of her head, still there but always pushed back. It all came down to societal pressures in the end: peers, mates, desires, and perceptions. Catherine had just pushed her out of her comfort zone, and that was as plain as daylight!

She was head over heels in lust with her. She had to tell her right now. Tell her she was certain of anything and didn't require any more time. Every second that Catherine could be relieved of her suffering, every second that she could soothe her aching core, counted. But first, she had to see to other matters.

Even though it was well past midnight, Catherine worked furiously on her mobile. First, she submitted an e-mail to her boss telling him that she would be out of the lab for a few days due to Canada's extended journey for personal purposes. She even called him first thing in the morning. After that, she went to the Air Canada website to book a trip to Toronto. She snagged a last-minute seat on a United Airlines flight to New York...and a return flight from Toronto via London Heathrow, but fucking hell! "Four thousand bucks, fucking?" "There goes my saving," she thought for a split second. Catherine had worked for so long that four thousand dollars were nothing in comparison.

Then she sent her parents an email telling them that she'd be landing at Toronto's Pearson at about 16:10 local time and asking them to pick her up kindly. She then packed a tiny carry-on suitcase, took a shower, and drank a large mug of hot, black coffee. She had a huge day ahead of her, and she wanted a jump start.

Catherine

Catherine has had a dreadful week. Her emotions were varying between melancholy and rage at her situation. Worse, she didn't have any courses or job load to distract her since it was the week before the start of the second semester. As a result, her mind replayed the incidents that lead up to the fateful night last Saturday. Had she expressed everything she ought to say? Or had she misplaced her temper and screamed at the wrong person? Was there something going on between them, or had she suffocated it by putting so much heat on Vanessa?
Worse, it was her birthday today, and she was not in the mood to get happy birthday phone calls from everyone. The last one

she needed to talk to was Vanessa, but she had seemingly disappeared without a trace. True, Catherine had advised her not to call or communicate with her until she had a clear response, but have not heard from her for a week was heartbreaking. Not just that, but her space was still dim as she passed beneath once or twice. She'd asked Alan about it casually, and he'd informed Catherine that Vanessa had left with a tiny travel bag quite early on Sunday morning.

She may have had a convention or something, Catherine reasoned, although she hadn't discussed something of the kind while they were talking last Saturday.

In any event, it was another Saturday, her birthday, and she didn't want to welcome the world. She had sat in her pajamas, turned off her cell, and unhooked her landline phone. She was idly playing with her iPad, which her parents had given her for Christmas, when she heard the familiar message that she had mail. She skipped it because she didn't want to read another canned happy birthday message from one of the several websites to which she was subscribing.

A couple of seconds later, another pipping sound alerted her to the arrival of new mail. And there was another. And yet another. She opened the application, irritated, to see who the spammer had been. There were four emails, both of which came from Vanessa.

Where have you gone? Your cell is turned off, and your landline is not operational.

Is it you, Catherine? Are you present? Please open the door. I'd like to speak with you.

Hello, Catherine. I know you're in there somewhere. Allan said that he did not see you leaving the property. Please, open up!

If just to send you a gift for your birthday, Anakin...

The most recent one was just a few seconds old. She hurriedly put on her slippers and dashed to the outside door of her staircase. She saw a shivering Vanessa pressing her palms together; her hat pulled over her ears.

"Who is Vanessa?"

"Catherine...ummm...could we...I mean..."

"Vanessa, I'm not in the mood for playing. What do you desire?"

Vanessa raised her head from the depths of her hoodie. When their gazes meet, Catherine noticed that her eyes gleamed in the same way that one's eyes glean when she's running a fever. Catherine's demeanor softened instantly. "Get inside, you stranger. You'll meet the demise waiting outside like that. Let's have you both bundled up here." Catherine embraced her friend and vigorously rubbed her shoulder.

Subzero conditions were not normal in England during the winter, although a cold front would sometimes blow in from the northeast, potentially dangerous. Vanessa's teeth were chattering; she had gone out in only her jeans and a hoodie, and she was shivering right now, in Catherine's bed. Catherine tucked a blanket around her and brought her a hot cup of tea.

"What on earth were you thinking? How long have you been waiting there outside?"

Vanessa raised her head, a puzzled smile on her lips as if assessing the circumstance, but she said nothing.

"I apologize for snapping at you. It's just...I've had a really bad week..."

"Just tell me about it..."

"Are you serious? What brought you here, Vanessa?"

Vanessa gazed into the whirlpool that was her teacup. "I told my parents...It didn't work out."

Catherine glanced at her, her face contorted in uncertainty. "What are you on about? What exactly do you mean you told them?"

Vanessa raised her head. "You know, you can be surprisingly thick for a wiz-kid at times. I told them about us." Vanessa continued, taking a deep breath, setting her teacup down, and standing eye to eye with Catherine. "I adore you, Catherine. I'm in love with you, and I'm not talking about the kind of love where we're best friends. I'm referring to romantic passion. I say love in the sense that I want to do things to you, erotic things...things that I'm not sure what I'd be doing, but something I've fantasized and dreamed about.

After our brief conversation on Saturday, I realized you were right. I couldn't keep saying we were all best friends any longer. So I asked myself some probing questions and went in search of answers. Let me reveal a little secret to you. You'll despise me when I'm done, but...here goes... I've had feelings for you for a long time... I didn't get what they were saying...when they wouldn't go, I wanted to run. It was my choice to come here to graduate... I just wished...prayed that being away from you would help this thing I was feeling go away.

I attempted dating, long-term marriages, and one-night stands...we all know how far those went. I assumed it was my fault that I was doing something wrong and mentally ill. And so you came along...you revealed your great secret to me that night... I was on the verge of kissing you...but I stopped myself.

Then...you came here, and I tried to stop you. I immersed myself in college, attempting to block you out of my thoughts. And then there was the Nora stuff... I was distraught, but I had just myself to blame... When you came into the office last week, and I hugged you in my arms as you screamed, I felt...indescribable... it's I felt so warm and full on the inside. And in the movies, while you did that cutesy thing with your head on my back...

You then traced a line in the desert. You took a stand...you got me out of my comfort zone...which was a positive thing because it forced me to consider.

Many of my reservations regarding being with you were in my mind about other people's expectations about me and what it implied. So I resolved to take control of it... I flew back to Canada last Sunday and told my parents about us...well, about me being homosexual... That didn't go too well...my father named me a variety of names... I wound up spending the night in a hotel... Oh well, I think you can't win them all..."

"You flew back to Canada, didn't you? You told your parents, right?"

"I simply followed the advice of a woman."

"Did that mean...you meant all of that?"

"No, I just made all of this nonsense up and wasted $5,000 on a red-eye flight for the sake of it. May I just get a fucking kiss and a hug right now?" Vanessa said with a wide smile on her lips.

Vanessa

Catherine's smile was as bright as the light. She swooped in and held her so tightly that she lost her breath. Soon, though, there were hands in the air and embraces being exchanged; there was a sense of urgency in the air that pushed them together. Catherine kissed her hungrily on the lips; Vanessa almost vanished as she saw Catherine's snake-like equivalent flick the underside of her tongue. She hissed and countered back, breathing through her nose.

Catherine's palms grazed her buttocks, pulling her pelvis down towards her thigh. Her jean-clad cunt humped against Catherine's thigh with a tantalizingly gradual burn; Vanessa could see everything down there swell up. She wasn't normally a torrential lubricator, even with her past boyfriends, she had to do a lot of foreplay to get warmed up, but this...this was a romantic encounter from another world! But this is how it's going to go down, she thought as she felt her panties dampen with her enthusiasm.

Meanwhile, Catherine's hands had moved upwards, fondling her breasts across the layers of fabric. Vanessa, sensing the hint, tugged on her hoodie, and clothes began to flap across the building. Catherine almost tore her pajamas as she struggled to pull them off. Both of them were soon stripped nude, with only the noises of their rapid breaths to be detected.

Catherine had come to a halt and was staring at her from head to toe. "This is our first time; I want to burn this picture to infinity," Vanessa replied, amused. Vanessa returned her stare. Catherine was a real beauty by all accounts. Her dark brown hair hung straight down to her shoulders. Behind black-framed frames, almond-colored eyes playfully hid. Her Mediterranean descent from her mother's side was evident in her wheat-colored eyes. Her breasts, despite being on the small side, protruded proudly in a traditional omega formation. What she missed in volume, she made up for in nipple size; her light pinkish-brown nipples stood entirely erect, surrounded by big, similarly colored areolas.

Her tummy was parallel to her body and revealed the soft contours of a six-pack, a testament to her rigorous preparation. Her legs were long and well-shaped from all of her racing. And her gaze lingered right where those long limbs started, where a lush triangle of pubic hair beckoned her. indicating the object of her attention and implying the lost treasure

They weren't idle for long. Catherine was all over her, pulling her back on her bed like a lion on its prey. Vanessa lay powerless, her legs half spread, her pulse beating madly out of balance, her breathing fired to smithereens. Catherine's body was resting between her thighs, making delicious contact with her throbbing cunt. Catherine paid tribute to her breasts by licking, kissing, and flicking her nipples with her incredibly agile tongue. "My God," was the only word that came out of her mouth as she stared enthralled at the silver path of kisses Catherine left in her wake.

Her cunt was leaking heavily by this stage, and she could feel it drip past her bum and onto the bedsheets. Catherine had to bite her lip down tightly to refrain from crying as her heated breath blew through her craving cunt. Catherine was now playing with her; she kissed the inner portion of her thighs and her outer lips, but she wouldn't move anywhere to where she desired her to be. "What do we have here? Hmmmmmmmmmmmmmmmmmmmmmmmmmmmmmm mmmmmmmmmmmmIs that a warm...wet...little butterfly spreading its wings just for me?" Catherine said in a sly tone. "I'm curious what we can do with it..."

"Oh, Catherineaaaaaaaaaaaaaaaaaaaaaaaaaaaaaaaaaaaaaaa

"Just tell me what?"

"Oh, for the love of fuck! If you want me to plead? I...huuuuuuuuuuuuuuuuuuuuuuuuuuuuuuuuuuuuuuuuuuuu"

When Catherine latched her lips on her clitoris, Vanessa went insane. "Oh my God...fuck...oh yes...right there...don't...don't stop...right there..."

Vanessa arched her back and raised the lower half of her body off the bunk. Catherine's firm hands gripped her buttocks and supported her waist. She was seconds removed from a star-bursting ecstasy and had a bird's eye view of it all.

Catherine created a suction-like sensation with her lips as her tongue twirled around her uncovered clitoris like crazy. Vanessa arrived as she'd never come before, her arms strained, her knees perched on the tips of her toes, and she grunted loudly. Her pulsating cunt sends huge shockwaves of previously unseen gratification. Catherine's gentler intercessions held her alive. Finally, her body exhausted like a firecracker, she slumped on the bed, unable to shift or think. Catherine gingerly lapped up her juices, gently sucking and slipping her tongue through the folds of her mouth, her eyes staring desperately at the ceiling.

Catherine leisurely paraded her tongue up and down, licking her outer lips, French-kissing the entrance to her vagina while still missing her oversensitive clitoris, and Vanessa lost track of time. However, after a moment, this languid lapping began to spice things up again, and she felt her body tremble with lust once more. Catherine continued the strokes with her lips, similar to how a cat laps up milk from a cup.

Then a finger made its way inside her, accompanied by another. She could feel them crook upwards, circularly massaging a certain region inside her. A wave struck her, but it wasn't the sharp, strong, cliff-like wave of her first orgasm. This was a gentler, larger wave that rumbled from deep inside her and seemed to go on indefinitely. Vanessa trembled like a rag doll.

"Oh fuck...fuck...fuck...what are you doing to me...what are you doing to me...what are you doing? Fuck you. Fuuuuuuuuuuuuuuuuuuuuuuuuuuuuuuuuuuuuuuuu "She cried as Catherine expertly coached the single drop of orgasmic energy from her. She figured she was done, but when Catherine swiped her clit with her tongue, it all began up again. Vanessa had lost count of when her second orgasm had finished, and her third had begun, or if this was just a massive roller-coaster ride.

"Oh, Jesus, Jesus! Oh my goodness...Fuck! Fuck!"

"That's got to be a world record for you. I've never seen you use the f-word so much."

"Stupid! You had me hang out with all those losers while we should have had THIS together? Oh my goodness! Talk about being self-centered!"

"I can just point you in the direction of the river, sweetie. Once there, you would drink on your own. You know...you can't create bricks until you have clay...yadayadayada..."

"I'm astounded that you can think of eloquent responses right now. To regain my mental faculties, I may need some kind of tonic."

"Oh? May I give it another shot?"

"No...no...no...no...no...no...no...no...no...no...no...n   But...I'm confident we'll have more time in the future..."

"Is it you, Vanessa? Do you believe that?" In a small speech, Catherine inquired.

"Yes, I do! Of course, I won't often be on the receiving end, and I'll have little idea what I'm doing. However, I'm certain I'll catch up. After all, we have a life ahead of us."

Conclusion

Winter of 2015

Catherine

"Can you kindly refrain from trotting ahead like a horse? With this dress and shoes on, I can't keep up with you. Why did we have to put these outfits on again?"

"Because the dress code requires it. Quit moaning and appreciate the view; that's why we're walking around a click in these, to take in the view from the bridge."

"It had better be fine, Anakin. The only thing they could not do at the gate was conducted a cavity scan. It's the first time they've asked for a printed copy of my hotel reservation one mile before the restaurant!"

"Oh, please whining! Aside from that, cavity search? Don't offer me any suggestions. It's bad enough that I have to tolerate your swaying butt and apparent lack of panties...don't make it any more difficult for me. I say it's already difficult not to be able to kiss you in public... Whose plan was it to celebrate our first anniversary in Dubai?"

"It was your concept, and this dinner reservation was also your idea. So stay still and drool still. I'll sway my a$$ as much as I want."

Despite their humorous banter, their fast speed enabled them to quickly cross the bridge connecting the mainland to the artificial island. The famed sail-like signature architectural marvel of Dubai, the Burj-al-Arab, stood directly in front of them. They were respectfully invited to wait in the lounge and offered a glass of water and a palm date while their reservation was registered. Dazzled, they glanced around; it was coated with gold plating as far as the eye could see. The building's interior provided the appearance of standing in aspire; internal balconies overlooked the central lobby, giving the interior a sense of vastness.

Soon after, the maître motioned for them to join him. Their reservation at the Junsui Far Eastern Buffet was registered, and they were led inside. As they arrived, they were greeted with another surprise: there were over a hundred and twenty oriental dishes, including Japanese, Thai, and Chinese cuisine, among others. The wine selection alone was some pages long! Talk about being overwhelmed! Catherine purchased a bottle of pink Moet champagne for them and suggested after their Swarovski flutes were filled:

"Well...then...to your good health, my princess."

Vanessa

Vanessa raised an eyebrow at her, thinking to herself, "to your good health?" but doing nothing. "Oh well...it would have been nice for her to propose...maybe later, when these damned waiters quit standing above our heads."

They loaded their plates once, twice, then a third time, but there was still no plan. The head waiter then recommended they pursue some freshly prepared Teriyaki-style beef.

"Oh, thank you so much. Hello, Leia! If you want to give it a shot?"

"No way! I'm not hungry anymore. I fear I'm going to burst if I take one more bite!"

"But...Teriyaki...is that your favorite? Can we maybe ask for anything else?"

"No, Catherine...come on...come on..."

"I was seven years old when my instructor taught me that the most colorful insects were often the nastiest, and I was sixteen when I stared into your blue eyes and knew he had been right all along. As a result...I'd like to extend my side... Can you be mine as much as you like me?"

On the table was a small diamond-studded platinum bracelet.

"Oh my God! ENTIRELY! YES, I DID!" Vanessa sobbed again, but this time it was cries of gratitude and pleasure.

CPSIA information can be obtained
at www.ICGtesting.com
Printed in the USA
BVHW091923200521
607797BV00002B/181